THE LONG AND THE SHORT OF IT

A Collection of Short Stories

RJ STASTNY

THE LONG AND THE SHORT OF IT
A COLLECTION OF SHORT STORIES

iUniverse books may be ordered through booksellers or by contacting:

iUniverse
1663 Liberty Drive
Bloomington, IN 47403
www.iuniverse.com
844-349-9409

ISBN: 978-1-6632-3496-4 (sc)
ISBN: 978-1-6632-4115-3 (e)

Library of Congress Control Number: 2022910906

Print information available on the last page.

iUniverse rev. date: 06/24/2022

CONTENTS

PREFACE

The eleven stories in this collection share no common theme other than that all of them own some experiential part of me. They're born out of an unequal mix of fact, fiction, and fantasy, and many of the characters are inspired by real people; many of the situations, by real experiences; and many of the places, by actual locations.

While the stories are short, I hope your reading enjoyment is long.

THE SWIM

*I*T WAS 6:45 A.M. RICHARD walked the short distance through the well-manicured garden to the swimming pool as he did every day since moving to the Desert Hot Springs Retirement Villa three weeks earlier. He would slowly swim the breaststroke until his fitness watch vibrated after exactly forty minutes. The pool was open to everyone at the villa, but he was the only one to swim at that time of the morning. In fact, most of the units were empty for half the year until the snowbirds returned for the winter months.

Richard had recently retired. He had never married and had no close friends. Suffering from social awkwardness since childhood, he considered himself a loner.

Pepín, an immigrant from Guatemala, was the gardener of the complex. He took meticulous care of the grounds and was always by the pool first thing in the morning when he made his rounds on Mondays and Fridays.

Pepín routinely would go about his chores, planting fresh flowers around the pool area, trimming bushes, and watering. From a distance, his youthful enthusiasm in the garden disguised the fact that he was older than Richard.

As time went on, Richard would pause near the end of the pool where Pepín was working and acknowledge the gardener with a nod. In subsequent weeks, he noticed that Pepín would wait until he neared the end of the pool to return the gesture.

After a while the nods were accompanied by smiles and occasional waves, the silent equivalent of *hello* and *hola*.

One day, Richard noticed that Pepín was gesturing with his face and hands to the plants while trimming off their spent flowers and dead leaves. To Richard's surprise, he cut one of the flowers and brought it to the end of the pool.

As Richard swam to the pool's edge, Pepín held the flower to his nose, then handed it quickly to Richard, who brought the flower to his face. He nodded to Pepín, acknowledging the sweet fragrance of the flower.

"Hello, I'm Richard." His voice was weak, as he was uncomfortable initiating conversation.

Pepín responded by pointing to his ears and his mouth and shaking his head. Richard nodded. He understood their communication would be silent.

When Pepín had bent over to hand him the flower, Richard couldn't help but notice the small garden shears hanging around his neck on a rawhide cord. The intricately carved metal handles of the shears glistened in the sun. Richard pointed and gave a complimentary nod. Pepín grinned and briefly held the shears against his chest.

Throughout the hot summer, both men remained loyal to their routines. Richard waited for his Monday and Friday swims with special anticipation. On those days he would purposely slow down when he reached the end of the pool, hoping to receive one of Pepín's floral gifts.

Given that they were strangers in a silent world, it was unlikely that either Richard or Pepín found it necessary to understand the unspoken relationship they had cultivated. Instead, they remained content to quietly enjoy the comfort of an uncomplicated companionship.

One Friday near the end of the summer, Richard went for his swim, anticipating the company of his quiet friend. But Pepín never showed up. For two weeks Richard looked for him, but Pepín didn't return.

He inquired with the retirement home manager, who informed him that Pepín no longer worked there. He had become very ill and was taken from the Valley Center for the Hearing and Speech Impaired, where he lived, to the local hospital.

On the following Monday immediately after his swim, Richard drove to a florist a few blocks away. He requested a small bouquet of flowers, insisting that he didn't care what kind they were as long as they were fragrant.

A short time later he walked in to hospital room 108 and approached Pepín's bedside. Imitating Pepín's poolside ritual, Richard held the flowers to his nose, then held them to Pepín's face. Tears ran down Pepín's sun-darkened cheeks as he breathed in the fragrance of the bouquet. Richard's eyes dampened as well.

For nearly three weeks, every Monday and Friday after his swim, Richard stopped by the florist and made the short pilgrimage to room 108.

One Friday, Richard arrived with flowers in hand, only to find an empty room.

The nurse on duty recognized Richard and handed him a large padded envelope marked "For Richard." She explained it was from Pepín's son, who lived several hours away.

Richard sat down and reached his hand deep inside the envelope. To his surprise, he pulled out the engraved shears that Pepín had always worn around his neck. He read the accompanying note:

> Dear Mr. Richard,
>
> > My father said your friendship and your visits to the hospital with the flowers gave him the greatest comfort when he needed it most. He felt you shared his passion for gardening and wanted you to have his pair of shears, which was a cherished gift from my grandfather in Guatemala many years ago.

Richard wiped the tears from his cheek and hung the shears around his neck as Pepín had worn them.

He finished reading the note:

> > Thank you, Mr. Richard, for being such a good friend to my father. I invite you to visit me sometime.
>
> > Sincerely, Pepín Bello Jr.
> > Oh, and I have a pool.

Richard picked up the flowers he had brought. He took a deep breath and held them to his face one more time.

SOUFIANE

"**I** GOT ACCEPTED!" WILL YELLED.

"Accepted for what?" his roommate responded from across the room.

"I'm one of four artists accepted to attend an artist retreat in Ordino, Andorra." Will could barely contain his excitement.

His roommate commented, "I thought Andorra was Samantha's mother in *Bewitched*."

Will shook his head. "No, stupid, that's Endora. And you just demonstrated why Americans have such a bad reputation for geography."

Will was the chief photographer for the *Windy City Gazette*, a monthly magazine serving the LGBTQ community in Chicago. He recently had won a grant based on a photo essay he did about gay politics in the Midwest. After he had read about organizations hosting retreats for artists of various genres, he decided to use his grant money to apply. His friends encouraged him but also cautioned how four artists confined to a small space for six weeks could be tantamount to lighting a fuse to a box of dynamite.

Will countered, "Well, battling egos and artistic melodrama might be good subject matter for my photos—that is, if I survive all six weeks." He was joking but also knew there was probably some truth to what they were saying.

Will arrived a day early to the small town of Ordino so he could get acquainted with the rustic host village. He thought Andorra, nestled in the Pyrenees Mountains between France and Spain, seemed like an exotic place to hold a remote retreat. He stayed at a small inn at the edge of town a couple of miles from the site of the retreat. The native language was Catalan, but French and Spanish were widely spoken. English was common only in tourist locations. Will spoke just enough Spanish to embarrass himself.

He spent a full day exploring the village, and while he found the villagers to be friendly, he couldn't help but notice their curious stares as he passed. His short, curly blond hair and six-foot frame stood out among the stocky, dark-haired natives of this Basque region.

It was late afternoon in the waning days of summer in the high country. Darkness came earlier, and nightfall was accompanied by rapidly falling temperatures. Will was eager to start his hike to the small house where he would join the other three artists.

Gathering up his limited belongings: a large backpack with his personal effects and a large duffel bag with his camera equipment, he followed the directions he had received from the retreat organizers. After a forty-five-minute walk along a dirt road and an encounter with a herd of sheep, he arrived at his destination. A sea of wildflowers nearly swallowed the small two-story house made of stone. He was tempted to take out his camera and start shooting the beautiful scenery but figured there would be time for that once he was settled.

Will knocked on the front door. There was no answer. From his backpack, he dug out the key that had been left for him at the village post office.

"Hello, is anybody here?"

The house was quiet. There was a small living room with a kitchen and dining table in the corner. The place was compact and sparsely furnished. Remembering what his friends had said, Will figured four strong personalities could quickly fill up the empty space.

The second floor had three bedrooms and one bath to be shared by all four visitors. Will's budget was tight, so instead of a private room, he had signed up to share a bedroom with another artist. He knew little about his future housemates other than their names and occupations from the roster he had received before he left Chicago: Errol, a choreographer from England; Delfina, a writer from Argentina; and Soufiane, a painter from Algeria, who also was Will's assigned roommate.

Will walked up the stairs to find his room and drop off his gear. The first two rooms were the singles. It didn't appear that either Errol or Delfina had arrived yet. The next room was his. It had two single beds with a large window in between that overlooked a huge meadow framed by mountains on all sides. Distracted at first by the magnificent view, Will noticed a huge trunk on the other side of the room on one of the beds, along with a backpack and duffel bag.

"Hmm, Soufiane," he mumbled, as he figured his roommate for the next six weeks had already checked in.

With little to unpack, Will went downstairs and found the kitchen stocked with some basics and enough for several meals until he and his roommates could agree on a menu and go to town to buy supplies. Coffee was all he needed at the moment.

He relaxed on the couch, waiting for the others to arrive.

First to come in was Errol, who was tall and thin as an asparagus spear. "Hello there, mate!" he announced with celebrity flair. "I'm Errol. You must be either Will or Soufiane."

"I'm Will. Nice to meet you. Did you have a good trip?"

"Not really. The flight attendant put a hold on my liquor the last hour. She was a nasty piece of work," Errol said, shaking his head. "And that bus drive up the mountain made me dizzy. Fortunately, the little market in town had my favorite vodka." Errol wasted no time looking for an empty glass in the kitchen so he could make himself a cocktail.

Will already was imagining what could lie ahead with a heavy drinker in the house.

A short while later, Delfina walked in. She was pulling a Louis Vuitton suitcase behind her and had a large matching shoulder bag. She was attractive, middle-aged, with flowing red hair that fell below her shoulders.

"Hello, gentlemen. That's quite a hike in these shoes. I guess I'll need to dress down a bit." Delfina had a mild Argentine accent but appeared to have a solid command of English.

Errol chirped in, "Honey, I can give you a few fashion

tips on how to be elegant and country at the same time." He threw the long red scarf he was wearing over his shoulder.

Delfina looked at him with a raised eyebrow. "*Perdóname, muchacho*, but I'm not anyone's honey."

The three of them chatted a bit before Errol and Delfina went upstairs to unpack. Will stayed downstairs, enjoying another cup of coffee and a pastry he had brought from town.

About an hour later, Soufiane walked in carrying a large shopping bag. He barely glanced at Will and walked directly to the kitchen to unload some groceries.

He was short, and his tight pants and sweater revealed a fit physique. He had a dark complexion, curly black hair, and a short black beard.

"Hello, I'm Will."

Soufiane didn't respond.

"Hi," Will tried again. "You must be Soufiane."

Soufiane finally acknowledged him and nodded. In a muted voice, he said, "Yes, I'm Soufiane."

Will assumed that his strong accent meant that his English might be limited. "Do you speak English, Soufiane?" he asked, at the risk of embarrassing Soufiane.

"Yes, enough to understand what I need to know." His answer seemed a bit abrupt. Will figured he'd need to be patient with his new roommate.

That evening, Errol, Delfina, and Will gathered in the living room.

Delfina suggested, "Why don't we have some wine and cook a light meal together? We can talk and get to know one another."

"Great idea! Let me run upstairs. I'll get my phone

and mini speakers so we can have some music." Errol spun around in a dance move and laughed. "We may as well make this a proper party!"

Delfina responded, again with her eyebrow arched, "Hmm, I don't think I'm ready to boogie down quite yet."

After Errol ran upstairs, Will confided to Delfina, "That's probably the choreographer blood in him." They both chuckled.

Delfina replied, "And I think there's something else in that blood too." She laughed.

Will ignored Delfina's comment and yelled upstairs, "Errol, ask Soufiane to come down and join us." He whispered to Delfina, "I think Errol's a little high. He brought his own bottle of vodka with him."

Errol came down the stairs alone. "What's with that bloke? I told him to bring his handsome self down here for cocktails and dinner. He gave me a dirty look and didn't say anything." Errol tripped on the last step but didn't fall.

Not wanting to waste an opportunity to throw some shade, Delfina commented, "Are you drunk, or is that one of your dance moves?"

Will interrupted before an argument could start. "Errol, Soufiane may not understand English that well, and you know, he's from Algeria and may be Muslim. You need to be a little more tactful." Will didn't feel comfortable playing referee on the first day, but remembering what his friends advised him about the fuse and dynamite, he hoped to reduce the tension.

"Whatever. OK." Errol wasn't shy about making a first impression, good or bad.

They opened a bottle of wine and sat around the small

dining table. Will said, "Wait a minute, I'm going to go up and see if I can get Soufiane to join us. We are going to spend six weeks here in this small house, and we need to get along."

"Listen, if he doesn't want to participate, let him stay to himself," Errol said with a little resentment in his voice.

Delfina shushed him by putting her finger to her mouth.

Will knocked on the partially closed door to their room. "Soufiane, it's me, Will. I wanted to make sure you're OK. It would be nice if you would join us. It's a good time for us to get to know one another. Do you understand?"

Soufiane came to the door. He didn't smile, but the scowl from his earlier interaction with Errol had left his face.

"And since we're roommates I hope we can be friends," Will added.

"OK, I'll be down in a minute," Soufiane replied.

Everyone had finished their first glass of wine before Soufiane made it down to the living room.

"Hey, mate, glad you finally made it," Errol said disingenuously.

Soufiane poured himself some juice he had bought at the market and sat at the table with the others.

"Well, why don't we go around the table and tell everyone a couple of things about ourselves, including why we're here." Delfina had already accepted the default position of leader of the house.

"I'll start," Errol said eagerly. "As I'm sure you all must know, I'm a well-known choreographer in Britain with many awards to my name and—"

Delfina shrugged her shoulders and tilted her head.

Errol childishly snubbed his nose at Delfina, then

11

continued. "And by the way, did you see the *Lion King*?" He giggled. "I gave those lion cubs all the moves. They wanted me to choreograph most of the show, but I had other commitments and—"

Delfina interrupted, saying, "OK, *mi niño*, now that you've given us the first chapter of your autobiography, why are you here?"

Errol returned another dirty look. "Well, my agent recommended I take a break, I mean sabbatical, to rejuvenate my creativity before the next big production."

Hoping to cool the tension between Delfina and Errol, Will asked innocently, "Oh, what show is that?"

Errol replied, "Uh, I don't know yet, but it's going to be big. And my wife and two kids are going to join me for a few weeks in Spain after this little party is over."

Delfina arched her eyebrow, a gesture that had already become her trademark expression of surprise and disdain. She muttered softly to herself, "Wife? Kids?"

She added, "All right, thank you, Errol. I guess we can expect a lot of tapping on the floor the next few weeks while you rehearse."

The sarcasm was not lost on Errol, who replied, "OK, so let's hear your fancy story, Ms. Vuitton," alluding to her taste in luggage.

Delfina explained that she had been asked by her literary agent to turn a short story she had written for a magazine into a full-length novel. "I thought a retreat like this might inspire me," she said.

"What is the story about, Delfina?" Will inquired.

"It's about a young homeless boy in a barrio of Buenos Aires who was adopted by one of Eva Perón's distant —"

Errol interrupted, saying, "Oh, I choreographed the stage version of *Evita*." He began singing "Don't Cry for Me Argentina."

"Don't worry, we won't!" Delfina cut in with some ferocity, clearly getting frustrated with Errol. She added, "I'm divorced, no children, and would like to travel through Spain for a short while after the retreat has ended."

"Oh, man hunting, I suppose," Errol said, determined to get under Delfina's skin.

"Well, don't worry, dear, we don't have the same taste, so I'm not your competition," she quipped with a scowl.

"I have a wife and kids!" Errol insisted, determined to reinforce the notion of his straight status. "And she tells me I quench her crazy."

Delfina shook her head and whispered, "I'm not sure I wanted to hear that."

Feeling the tension in the room, Will got up to look for the thermostat as he was feeling a chill—and it wasn't just the temperature.

"OK, who is next in this little tell-all exercise?" Delfina asked, directing the conversation.

Will replied, "Soufiane, do you want to say something about yourself?"

Soufiane had been sitting quietly, mostly staring across the room toward the window right behind Will. Occasionally, Will found his eyes locking momentarily with Soufiane's, but Soufiane quickly glanced away.

Appearing a little self-conscious from the eye contact, Soufiane said, "No, please go ahead."

Errol, who had walked to the kitchen for some water, turned around and said in a prosecutorial tone, "Why is he here if he doesn't want to participate?" He then said softly, but loud enough so everyone could hear him, "Is there something wrong with him?"

Will quickly interrupted, giving Errol a dirty look. "I'll go." He looked across at Soufiane, whose face was turning red.

Will explained that he was single and was a photographer for an LGBTQ magazine in Chicago. He had decided to use some grant money to join the retreat and focus on a different aspect of photography, namely, landscape.

Delfina leaned over to Will and said, pointing toward Errol in the kitchen, "LGBTQ magazine? And I would have guessed that he was the gay one, not you." She gave Will a warm smile and a wink.

Will, a little bothered by Delfina's falling in to the stereotype trap, whispered, "We come in all flavors, Delfina. Be careful before you judge."

Delfina nodded. "You're right. I'll apologize. But I'm still going to kick his ass when he's out of line."

After listening to Will, Soufiane became more attentive and raised his head to say, "Will, it must be rewarding for you to work for a magazine like that. I mean, the freedom to—"

Before Will could respond, Errol blurted out, "He speaks!"

Soufiane shouted angrily, "Yes, and I speak Spanish, French, and Arabic too!"

Errol was at a loss for how to respond.

Delfina, impressed with her polylingual housemate, turned to Will and quietly said, "Indeed, never rush to judgment."

Will turned to Soufiane. "Ignore him. And yes, the

magazine has a fifty-year history of activism and support for the LGBTQ community, and I'm proud to be a part of it. While there is still progress to be made in America, our community has come a long way in having our rights recognized."

Soufiane nodded. "I'd love to come to America someday."

Errol interrupted again, saying, "OK, it's Souffie's, or however you say it, turn."

"Shut up, Errol." Will had lost his patience with the choreographer. "All right, Soufiane, go ahead."

Soufiane glanced at everyone and then said slowly in a soft voice, "I'm a refugee from Algeria. I paint. A woman in Spain sponsored me to come here."

Errol started to say, "Oh, and are you her—"

Will held up his hand to Errol, signaling him to be quiet.

"Well, I think that's enough for now. I'm sure we'll get to know more about one another as time goes on. Six weeks and counting." Delfina seemed to enjoy her self-appointed role as master of ceremonies.

Over the next two weeks, everyone tried to settle in and focus on their art. While tensions between Soufiane and Errol were ever present, Soufiane did his best to avoid Errol.

Delfina and Errol spent most of their time in their rooms, she writing, and Errol—well, no one was really sure.

Will took long daily hikes, exploring the village and the countryside, taking photos, and returning with dinnertime accounts of some of the amazing landscapes he had photographed and the people he had met.

Soufiane had set up a little studio area in an enclosed side porch where he could paint.

As roommates, the two men could not avoid interacting with one another, and while reserved, Soufiane slowly warmed to Will. "Thank you for standing up for me. I don't like that Errol guy. He's mean." Soufiane's stoic and serious demeanor was betrayed by a small smile that spread across his face. Will was hoping it was a sign that Soufiane was becoming more comfortable with him.

Soufiane always kept the porch door locked while he was painting in his studio, primarily to prevent unwanted intrusions by Errol, whose art critiques were anything but generous. One day, Will came back early from one of his hikes and knocked on the door. Soufiane didn't answer. Will turned to walk back to the kitchen.

"Hey, Will, did you need something?" Soufiane asked in his quiet voice, having poked his head out the door.

"Oh, not really. Sorry to bother you. I just thought you might want to take a break some time and go on a hike with me."

To Will's surprise, Soufiane replied without hesitation, "Yes, I would like that."

Soufiane waved him in to come and see his studio.

Soufiane had one painting finished and was working on a second. Both works were done in tones of gray and brown. The first was a scene of people toiling in the street in a run-down neighborhood. Some subjects were sweeping the streets; others were carrying large bags of goods. Still others were gathered around large oil drums with small fires burning. While Will was impressed with Soufiane's Monet-like technique, he felt the tone was dark. The scenes were colorless and without joy. The slumping posture of the subjects added to a feeling of quiet sadness.

Will kept his comments to a minimum. "You're very talented, Soufiane."

Soufiane began to join Will on hikes several times a week. At first they didn't talk much, but Soufiane seemed to enjoy Will's company as he would occasionally tell Will how refreshing it felt to be out in the open country.

One afternoon, they were sitting on a stone outcrop overlooking the valley, about to return to the house, when Soufiane asked, "Will, can I tell you something?"

"Of course, Soufiane." Will noticed a nervous crackle in his voice.

"I appreciate your company. I feel relaxed around you. Thank you."

"You're welcome. You can hike with me anytime. And if there's anything you ever want to talk about or need, just ask." Will sensed there was more Soufiane wanted to say but didn't press him to talk.

"Thank you, Will."

Soufiane began to join Will more frequently on his hikes. While their conversations were mostly about the things they saw while on the trail, Will noticed that his companion was becoming more talkative. Soufiane would comment on how beautiful the wildflowers were and reminisce about the Algerian countryside where he grew up. Will realized that Soufiane's English was much better than he had first thought.

Occasionally, the group would gather together for dinner and talk about the progress of their respective projects.

Not surprisingly, Errol was usually the first to talk. "It looks like a big deal is in the works for me back in London. I've been choreographing scenes for a new musical."

Trying to sound genuinely interested, Delfina asked, "And how do you choreograph in your room without other dancers?"

"I sketch out scenes. The individual steps will be detailed out once I return to London," he explained.

Delfina said, "OK, I don't know how that works, but if you say so." She then explained that she was almost done with the first draft of her book. Errol could be heard humming the theme from *Evita* while she spoke.

Will reported that he'd been building a portfolio of photos—"portraits of a village," he called it.

When it came to Soufiane, Errol blurted out in a snarky tone, "How are the two hiking mates doing? Bonding brothers now?"

Soufiane stood up in a rage. "Shut the fuck up, you little worm. You have no respect for anyone else here. You're constantly trying to compensate for the loser you really are."

Soufiane went to his studio and slammed the door.

Everyone was surprised by his sudden but justified expression of outrage toward Errol and the latter's insinuation about Soufiane's friendship with Will, regardless of how accurate it may have been.

That evening, Will spoke with Soufiane in their room before bed. Soufiane apologized for his outburst but didn't want to talk about it.

"Soufiane, you don't need to apologize. You said what the rest of us were thinking. Errol is a fool."

"Thanks, Will. I just don't know if I can stay. I don't feel welcome here. Errol reminds me of the taunts I received in Algeria." Soufiane went to bed and buried himself under the sheets.

"I'm here for you, my friend, if you want to talk." Will tried to reassure him but realized that Soufiane was troubled and needed to free himself of whatever demons were haunting him.

The next morning when Will woke up, he noticed that Soufiane had already left. He went downstairs to Soufiane's studio and found it odd that it was unlocked, with no sign of him. While glancing at his paintings, Will noticed a piece of paper attached to the canvas of his unfinished work.

After he read what was on it, he sat in a chair and gasped. "Oh my God."

Soufiane had written a short poem.

> I'm the blues in the dark
> Carrying a burden of low somber notes,
> Slow vibrations of bass in my soul.
> And finally, I welcome the silence.

Will jumped to his feet and ran out of the house, heading down the familiar path of one of Soufiane's favorite hiking routes.

After fifteen minutes of running as fast as he could, Will arrived at the rock outcrop where they had sat on their first hike. He noticed a rubber wristband on the ground that Soufiane always wore that said, "I am free when all are free." But there was no sign of Soufiane. Fearing he had jumped, Will carefully leaned over the ledge and looked at the giant boulders hundreds of feet below. He saw nothing.

He called out in all directions, "Soufiane! Soufiane! It's me, Will. Soufiane, where are you? Soufiane!"

Distraught, with tears streaming down his face, Will

yelled until he was exhausted. He sat on the ledge for a couple of hours. No Soufiane.

As dusk approached, Will walked back to the house with his head slumped over his sagging shoulders. He went to the kitchen, pulled a fresh bottle of wine out of the fridge, and poured a glass.

Delfina was sitting on the couch, writing. "What's wrong, Will? You look exhausted and upset. Where were you?" Accustomed to seeing both Will and Soufiane return from their hikes together, she pressed, "Where's Soufiane?"

"I don't know, Delfina. I think he ran away." He shared the poem he had found in Soufiane's studio.

"Ay, Díos mío!" she exclaimed, putting her arm around Will. "Do you think he would harm himself?"

"I don't know. I looked all over for him. I feel responsible. I knew he was troubled, but he wouldn't open up."

Delfina consoled him as best she could. "It's not your responsibility or fault, Will. You made yourself available to him."

"But sometimes that's not enough, Delfina. He needed my help, and I think I know why." Will teared up again. As he looked around, he was grateful that Errol wasn't there. He wouldn't have been able to deal with him at that moment.

Will poured Delfina a glass of wine, then took his glass and the bottle up to his room. He drank until he fell asleep.

He didn't know how long he had been asleep when he was awakened by the sound of something being knocked over and falling to the floor. He turned the light on next to his bed. Squinting from the light, he said, "Oh my God, it's you, Soufiane!"

Soufiane sat down on Will's bed and started to cry. Will

put his arm around him. "Soufiane, I thought you had done something terrible."

"I was going to, Will. Sometimes I feel like a stranger in my own dreams—dreams filled with monsters and mayhem—and then I wake up to a world not much different."

Will didn't know what to say but continued to embrace him.

Soufiane continued, "I figured there was no one who would miss me. Certainly not my family, or my country, or people like Errol. And then I thought of you. I could not leave this world and disappoint the one person I felt had some faith in me."

Will gave Soufiane a kiss on the cheek then suddenly realized he may have crossed a boundary. "I'm sorry. I don't know why I did that."

"It's OK, Will. I think I know why." Soufiane returned the kiss.

Will quietly snuck down to the kitchen to steal another bottle of wine and a glass for Soufiane. They stayed up the rest of the night talking.

Soufiane opened up. "Will, the reason I fled Algeria was because my father kicked me out of the house and my older brother wouldn't talk to me. The neighbors harassed me and threatened me."

"I'm so sorry," said Will.

"You see, being different in Algeria is not the same as being different in America. People like me and you are thought of as criminals. I felt guilty because my father was wealthy by Algerian standards and he paid for a quality university education for me. I disgraced him and my family."

Soufiane's voice trembled as he continued. "My mother was the only one who showed me love. She would always say, 'Sami'—her nickname for me was Sami ever since I was a little boy—'Sami, no one is better than you. Believe in yourself.' She died when I was at the university. Ever since, I've felt I don't have a home to go to."

Will just sat and shook his head while Soufiane continued.

"I fled to southern Spain on one of the migrant boats. For a while I lived on the streets and drew caricatures of tourists for money to live on. Then a young woman who had a gallery began talking to me and asked if I had done any serious work. After I showed her some sketches, she thought I had potential as an artist. I worked at her gallery for a short time. Since I didn't really have a place to stay, she decided to sponsor me in this retreat with the agreement that I would return with some paintings she could show and, hopefully, sell. She told me it might also hold off immigration officials and give me time to file proper paperwork. I agreed. I had nothing to lose."

For the remaining three weeks of the retreat, Will and Soufiane were inseparable except for when Soufiane was painting. Their hikes gradually became joyous excursions, during which time they shared their life stories and dreams.

During one hike they stopped and rested at the rock outcrop. Will turned to Soufiane and asked, "Soufiane, what do you want most in your life?"

Soufiane replied without hesitation, "I want to feel peace. I want somewhere to call home." He turned to Will. "And you?"

Will replied, "I want to fall in love."

"You've never been in love?" Soufiane asked with a look of surprise.

"Not really. I think when you're really in love, you're willing to sacrifice anything for someone, and I've never felt that way until …" Will didn't finish his sentence.

Soufiane's and Will's eyes locked. They exchanged a passionate kiss. They said nothing. They didn't have to.

During their hikes, Soufiane would pick a small bouquet of wildflowers to bring back to brighten up the studio.

Will began to notice that his paintings began to include more colorful and joyful scenes. His works eventually became beautiful expressions of a new sense of self and freedom.

Will started taking a series of photos of Soufiane and his artwork. He had an idea.

A couple of weeks before the retreat was to end, Will said, "Soufiane, I want to ask you something. I would like to do a photo essay about you, your art, and your struggle to leave Algeria. I want to make you the focus of that piece. What do you think?"

"That's amazing. I would be honored, Will." Soufiane gave Will a big hug.

With the retreat wrapping up, everyone exchanged emails and cell phone numbers on the last night. Errol left the next morning without saying goodbye to anyone, although he did leave a note apologizing for his behavior. He admitted that he actually had been fired from his job in London and had taken his frustration out on them. He had hoped that the retreat would help him find some direction.

Delfina embraced Soufiane and Will.

"Stay in touch, my lovely amigos. I love you both."

Will and Soufiane spent an hour alone in the house together before leaving. They sat on the front step holding hands. Neither one really knew how to say goodbye.

Finally, Will broke the silence. "Soufiane, one thing I've learned while spending time with you in the peace of these mountains and pastures is that love grows in the quiet times. And I've grown to love you very much."

Soufiane replied with a long kiss. They wiped one another's tears that were running down their cheeks. They promised to stay in touch with the hope of meeting again, despite knowing that there was a good possibility such a reunion might not ever occur given the uncertainty of Soufiane's immigration status.

Soufiane returned to the gallery in Spain with half a dozen paintings. Will returned home and started work on his photo essay of Soufiane.

Will kept in touch with Delfina, who agreed to edit the draft of the magazine article for him. She told Will that she had heard that Errol never went back to London. Instead, he was living in Marbella, Spain, with his wife and kids. It was a big vacation destination for Brits, and he was teaching dance to tourists. Will thought to himself, *Man, that's a bit of irony. Now Errol's the one entertaining tourists, not Soufiane.*

A few weeks later, Soufiane sent Will an email explaining that his gallery showing was a big success and he had earned a substantial sum from the sale of his paintings. Will shared his news that he had pitched his piece to the magazine and they decided to make it the cover story of their next issue.

He asked Soufiane if he would be able to visit Chicago around the time of publication, but Soufiane lamented that he was still working on straightening out his immigration papers. He was very fearful that the Spanish authorities would follow through on their threat to deport him back to Algeria.

Will and Soufiane communicated regularly, hoping for a day when they would again meet and embrace. Will was comforted knowing that Soufiane's name meant "pure and devoted" in Arabic, but he shared his fear about potential deportation.

Will mailed Soufiane and Delfina copies of the magazine article, and Delfina announced the release of her novel. Soufiane shared photos of his gallery exhibition.

Two months passed. Will was in a meeting with magazine staff and noticed a call coming from Soufiane on his cell phone. He wasn't able to answer the call and was concerned because they usually texted or emailed one another. As soon as the meeting ended, Will listened to the voice mail message.

"Will, call me. It's urgent!"

Two weeks later, with a small bouquet of flowers in hand and tears streaming down his face, Will watched as a brown curly headed man, bounding with joy, ran toward him down the concourse at Chicago's O'Hare International Airport.

They embraced. Overcome with emotion, they were unable to speak.

Soufiane fought through the tears. "Will, I'm finally…" He couldn't finish.

Will kissed him. "Yes, Sami, you're home now."

THE HILL

$\mathcal{L}$IFE OFTEN LEADS US IN directions we may not
otherwise have chosen. I found myself retired, alone
in the desert. I was no longer at the job I enjoyed and
was miles away from friends I cared for. But there was one
person whom I promised I would regularly return to visit.

During the past two years, I met Kevin every few months
at the same place, a hill in the Santa Monica Mountains
overlooking the San Fernando Valley. Kevin and I had been
almost inseparable the past two decades, until I moved from
Los Angeles to the desert. It got harder to visit as the drive
could be tedious at times, yet it was important to me—to
both of us, I hoped.

I arrived midafternoon and grabbed the cooler from the
car. I usually packed a lunch for us. It took me about five
minutes to climb the hill, occasionally stopping to enjoy
the view, which was quite something when it was clear.
It had always been a favorite spot of Kevin's, a panorama
of suburbia below with the San Gabriel Mountains in the

distance. The mountains were all that separated the heat of the desert from the city.

"Hey, Kev, it's great to be with you again. I know I'm late. That drive in from the desert took longer than expected today."

I spread the blanket that I always brought on the moist grass. From my backpack I took out our favorite lunch—a bottle of wine and sandwiches.

"I hope the wine is still cold." I poured two glasses and made a toast to my very special friend. "Here's to what we will always share, regardless of distance and the different directions life has taken us."

I sipped from my glass, sighed, and turned toward Kevin. "Yes, I've been OK. I'm still adjusting to retirement. Meeting friends in a new city is a challenge, but what choice do we have, right?"

I described the hikes I regularly took on the relatively deserted desert trails with my adopted chocolate Lab, Zigzag. "You'd love the one trail I found. It leads to a small lagoon, a true oasis. Zigzag always runs ahead of me, eager to plunge in to the water." Kevin loved the outdoors too, and we were both disappointed when our tent trailer we had bought together years earlier was stolen.

I opened the sandwiches, which I had neatly wrapped to keep them fresh on the long drive—turkey for me and a hot link for Kevin.

It was an unusually clear afternoon for typically hazy Los Angeles. Looking toward the horizon, I could make out the fire tower on the distant mountain range.

"Kev, do you see that? Remember when we used to hike up there? I'll never forget when we got caught in a strong thunderstorm and we thought we were going to get washed down the mountainside. You blamed me for months for not checking the weather report." I chuckled.

I took a couple of bites of my sandwich and washed it down with some wine. "I guess we've survived a lot of adventures, not the least of which was the brush fire that came awfully close to where we both lived years ago. And then that time the earthquake knocked down a telephone pole and just missed your car."

I continued, "A couple of weeks ago Richard asked me if we were still meeting on the hill. I told him that as long as I'm only a few hours away, I'll do everything I can to maintain our reunions."

Richard was a good friend of ours who had introduced us almost twenty years ago.

"Richard told me that he'd like to join us sometime. I told him I thought you would like that."

The truth was, I cherished these private visits and was reluctant to share them with anyone else.

I refilled my wineglass, as I did several times during our visit.

We sat in silence for a while. I laid my head down and moved as close to him as I could. I looked up at the clouds and watched them quickly pass overhead until I dozed off, sleeping for a good thirty minutes at least.

During my short nap I dreamt about the cross-country car trips Kevin and I loved to take. We were on the highway in the middle of Utah, talking for what seemed like hours, laughing, weighing in on major world problems, and making big decisions such as what time to pull over for the night. I mentioned I was hungry, and he popped open a Diet Coke and filled my free hand with peanuts, generously refilling it when it was empty. We laughed as a van passed us covered in "The End Is Near" stickers. He leaned over, gave me a quick kiss, and said, "Guess I'd better kiss you now. You never know."

A warm gust of wind blew over me, and I woke up to a sweet scent in the air. I felt a tear running down my cheek.

"Do you smell that? I remember you loved that smell. It always reminded you of the jasmine growing along the fence in your mother's backyard."

As I ate the rest of my sandwich, I suddenly remembered something. "Oh, I almost forgot." I pulled a bag out of my backpack and opened it. "Here's a small bouquet of gardenias. They were hard to find because they're getting out of season at the florist. But I know you wouldn't be happy without your favorite flower." I laid them by his side. I think he was pleased.

I turned toward him and asked, "Kev, do you mind if I sell the house in the desert? I know it was to be our eventual dream home, and I really hate to give it up, but it's too much work just for me." I had dreaded bringing up this topic, but I would leave that day with the matter settled.

The cool of the late afternoon was tempered by the sense of warmth that the companion next to me provided. It was more than warmth; it was what the Brazilians call *saudade*—a feeling of melancholy and nostalgia, a desire for something that may not always be present.

I relished my moments on the hill. It was the in-between times that were difficult, when the darkness I thought I had left behind crept back in. At times, I wasn't sure if there was any happiness left for me. These moments on the hill replenished the love that I was desperately afraid of losing by living alone in the desert. I remained by Kevin's side for a while longer, wanting to feel his peace fade into me.

Suddenly, from behind, there was another voice. "Sir, the gates close in twenty minutes. You can leave the flowers here. We'll pick all of them up on the weekend."

I sat up and told Kevin I had to drive back before it got too late. Our visit had passed so quickly that dusk was sweeping across the city like a giant blanket.

I grabbed his uneaten hot link and put it in my bag. I quickly drank the wine from his still full glass.

Kneeling by his side I told him, "The stars don't shine because of you, but you are the reason I look up at them."

As dusk approached, I looked up, and an invisible cloud of sweet jasmine passed over us. I knew he'd visit my dreams again.

*　　*　　*

THE AUTHOR'S MUSE

The hardest story to write is often your own.

In the 1980s, the ferocity of the AIDS epidemic left me one of the few survivors of a generation of close friends, including my partner, my dentist, my doctor, and my barber. The list could go on. Their lives were extinguished so quickly that there was little time to grieve. Occasionally, the memories bring joy, but often their weight crushes like a landslide.

I often struggle between guilt for having survived, anger

for having felt abandoned, and gratitude for having outlasted the dangers of life's great adventure for a few more decades.

While I'm grateful for some wonderful new friends who have come into my life, those from my young adulthood left me so early that we were unable to share the joys of reaching middle age together.

We all experience grief and loss. It leaves an emotional trail of holes and empty spaces, and sometimes trying to fill those holes is like pouring water into a fishnet. I've resigned myself to believing that those perforations are left unfilled on purpose, so we can celebrate the bright light that used to occupy those spaces.

Life repeatedly has taught me that forever isn't. But I take solace in knowing I'm a better man for having had people in my life so worthy of being missed, and it is to them that I dedicate "The Hill."

UNDERCOVER ROSE

*T*HE LAST OF THE PARTYGOERS had left except for Terry's best friend, Roberto. They had worked in the Peace Corps together in Peru for three years. Terry had left the United States and joined the Peace Corps Response Unit for a special management assignment shortly after his partner died in a car crash. He needed to escape the tragic memories and do something completely different. But now he felt it was finally time to go back home. He decided to go back to the Midwest, namely, Illinois, where he had been invited to teach botany and biology at a small college.

His Peace Corps colleagues, disappointed that he was leaving, surprised him at his house with a farewell party. Terry wasn't one who delighted in too much attention. While they teased him about how his full beard made him look like a young Chuck Norris, his personality was quite the opposite—borderline shy and soft-spoken. It was an emotional moment for him to say goodbye to the wonderful people from several different countries with whom he had bonded.

"Roberto, I sure hope I'm doing the right thing," Terry confessed. He looked sad as he admired the garden in his patio that he nurtured for the past three years.

Terry lamented, "My one-year mission turned in to three. I had fully expected that after one year I'd be ready to go home, but this feels like home now."

Roberto was from Chile. At age forty-eight, he was nearly ten years older than Terry. He was his closest friend on the Peace Corps team.

Much shorter than Terry's six feet three inches, Roberto had to reach up to put his arm around Terry's shoulder. "Listen, you've always said you want go back to teach again, but you know, they love you here and the regional director would welcome you back anytime."

Roberto's voice took on a more serious tone. "Terry, just remember what we talked about. Be careful when you get home. You're going to experience some culture shock, and many people won't be able to relate to your experience here. And you'll likely find that you're not the same Terry as the one who left three years ago. Life will never be quite the same. You may have left the mission, but the mission may not have left you. 'Ghosts' are everywhere."

"I get it. But I doubt those ghosts would want anything to do with me." Terry laughed, but he knew Roberto was serious.

Ghosts was the term some of the Peace Corps leaders employed to describe CIA operatives who worked throughout South America. Terry was based in the capitol city, Lima, which was home to many foreign embassies, including that of the United States and, of course, those of some of its adversaries. It was well-known that the CIA employed many of its operatives under official cover in the embassies and high-level organizations.

While the Peace Corps was apolitical, Terry's regional director unofficially advised staff to be careful of who they met, either casually or as part of their work. Terry managed a group of volunteers who supported a new ecotourism effort by the Peruvian government. Terry and Roberto, like many of the corps team members, had regular access to senior Peruvian officials. Operatives of the CIA and other foreign intelligence agencies were always trying to recruit agents with that kind of access who could provide information that could aid in many of their covert initiatives. It was also no secret that the Chinese were trying to influence the government at all levels.

Neither Terry nor Roberto had ever claimed they had been approached by the CIA, and they often joked about waiting for their 007 moment. Still, Terry trusted that Roberto knew what he was talking about and took his warning seriously. In the early 1970s, Roberto's father was recruited by the CIA as an agent in Chile in support of the ouster of Salvador Allende from power. It also was rumored that the previous Peace Corps director in their office had been compromised, which was why their current boss was being overly cautious.

Roberto gave Terry a firm hug. "Che, I'll be by early in the morning to take you to the airport."

The use of the word *che* was common in South America and Spain. The diminutive expression was used like "Hey, friend," "Hey, man," or "Hey, bro." When Terry and Roberto exchanged emails in the field, Roberto always ended his with "Che," indicating all was well.

After all the guests had left, Terry retrieved a beer from the fridge and went out to the patio for one last time. He inspected his rose garden and took a deep breath to smell the flowering vines that nearly covered the brick wall enclosing the patio. He listened to the tree frogs sing their evening songs.

Terry was flattered by the outpouring of support. In the midst of the tearful goodbyes, he knew some of the warm friendships he had developed would last for years to come. If only he knew to what extent this would be true.

The crew's announcement of their approach to Chicago's O'Hare airport woke Terry. It had been a long flight back to the States with a change of planes in Miami. Treating his arrival like one of his projects back in Peru, he had already made a list of things he needed to get done right away. First among them was to look for a permanent place to live as hotel expenses would add up quickly.

The college where he would be teaching was in a very affluent area, and he knew he couldn't afford to live there. After all, the salary and savings that afforded him a comfortable lifestyle in Peru would not go nearly as far in the States. Terry began to inquire about real estate agents.

Only a few days after his arrival, he received a surprise phone call on his cell number.

"Hello, is this Terry Davis?"

"Yes. Who may I ask is calling?"

"My name is Teresa Escobar. I'm a real estate agent. Roberto Ramos referred you and told me you would be looking for a home to rent or purchase in the area."

There was an awkward silence. Terry was surprised that his friend hadn't told him about contacting the realtor.

"Hello?" Teresa repeated.

"Oh yes, I'm sorry. I guess you caught me by surprise." Terry tried to sound apologetic but remained a bit mystified by the call. "Yes, yes. It is rather urgent I find a place quickly. I'll be teaching at Forest College in a few weeks and won't have too much time to look for places once I start work."

Without hesitation, Teresa responded, "Well, Roberto mentioned you were starting a new job, and if you're interested, I have some thoughts on a nice area that's not too far from the college yet is very nice and affordable. Would you like to—"

Still experiencing some anxiety about the surprise call, Terry cut her off midsentence. "Excuse me, but how do you know Roberto?"

"I'm sorry, but I thought maybe he would have told you about me. We were good friends at the university in Chile years ago, and our families are close."

With some relief in his voice, Terry responded, "Well, sure. Why don't we meet for lunch?"

"Great!" Teresa responded enthusiastically. "Are you free tomorrow? Let me know where you're staying. I can pick you up at your hotel."

Terry gave her his information and added, "I look forward to meeting you, Teresa, and getting started on my house search."

After hanging up, Terry was still a bit bewildered by how fast things were moving and that Teresa already knew so much about him. But he wasn't about to complain. That evening, he emailed Roberto to thank him for the referral.

He received a short reply: "You're welcome. Good luck, Che."

They hadn't really spoken much since his return, so Terry was disappointed by such a brief reply. *Oh well,* he thought, *Roberto is busy. I should be grateful for him going out of his way to help.*

The search didn't last long as Teresa immediately introduced Terry to a nice quiet neighborhood of small but well-kept homes on large wooded lots. It was only a twenty-minute drive from the college and was adjacent to the Great Lakes Naval Base. Teresa showed Terry a nice modest Cape Cod cottage for sale. While they walked up the sidewalk, Terry could hear an early morning bugle call from the nearby naval base. Normally, he would have spent several more days house hunting, but the home was exactly what he had in mind. It was a small two-story cottage surrounded by large oak trees. The street dead-ended at a large wooded area that bordered the base.

"Let's go for it!" Terry exclaimed. "I can't believe you found this so quickly. I hope they accept the offer."

Teresa responded with confidence, "Oh, they will. The seller has already vacated, and movers will be picking up their furnishings in the next few days. I'm quite sure there won't be any problems with your offer."

Teresa was right. Within three weeks, Terry was ready to move in to his house. He had only a few basic furnishings shipped from Peru and hurriedly purchased a couch, a kitchen table, and bedroom furniture.

Moving day arrived. As Terry met the shipping company in the driveway, he was approached by a young man in a navy uniform.

"Hi, I'm Kenji. I live next door." He pointed to the small

yellow house with children's toys scattered about the front lawn and a large black SUV in the driveway.

"Hello, I'm Terry. Nice to meet you. Navy man, eh?"

"Yes, sir. My family and I are just renting. You know the military, always on the move. I know you're busy getting settled. Just wanted to say hello."

Kenji's young son Evan ran up to Terry and said, "Hi, mister. You going to live here? Are you a spy too?" Kenji turned away from Terry, obviously caught off guard by his son's remarks. "Shush, Evan. Go inside. Your mother is making lunch for you."

"Great. Well, again nice to meet you, Kenji." Terry didn't react to the exchange, thinking his neighbor's son was just being a kid. He was relieved that his first encounter had been friendly. *Like they always say, you can't choose your neighbors*—or so he thought.

After the truck finished unloading the few possessions he had shipped from Peru, Terry opened one of the beers from a cooler and sat down on a box in the garage. He glanced around. The garage was empty but for a few odds and ends left by the previous owner. It just needed a good sweeping. As he picked up a broom, a gruff and gravelly voice startled him from behind: "Hello there."

Terry turned around quickly only to find himself face-to-face with an older bearded man wearing thick-lensed glasses. His pipe filled the air with the smell of sweet tobacco.

"Hi," Terry said in a cautious voice. "I'm Terry. I'm just moving in."

"Yeah, I guessed that. I'm Clint, your neighbor." He pointed to the larger two-story house on the other side. "Welcome to the neighborhood."

Terry replied, "Thanks. I was working for the Peace Corps in Peru for several years."

"Hmm." Clint took a puff on his pipe. "Oh yeah, I know there's a lot going on down there."

Terry thought it was a rather strange response, but Clint, by first appearances, seemed a bit odd anyway. Terry reached out to shake his hand, but Clint didn't reciprocate. Instead he fiddled with his pipe. Terry, noticing that Clint's hands were badly scarred, tried not to stare.

"What are you doing here?" Clint played with his pipe and didn't seem all that interested in the answer.

Terry responded, "I'll be teaching an ecology course at Forest College."

"Oh yeah. That figures. Well, I'll let you be. I'm sure we'll chat again."

Terry thought, *What does he mean, "that figures"? Well, he's different, that's for sure.*

Clint lumbered down the drive, the smoke from his pipe trailing behind him. He hadn't even made it down the driveway when his wife, Sharon, ran up with a container of chocolate chip cookies. The opposite of Clint, she could have been anyone's grandmother. She welcomed Terry to the neighborhood and then was gone as quickly as she had appeared.

Terry thought, *I've barely been inside my house and the neighbors have already descended.* He found Clint's surprise appearance a bit off-putting at first but figured he was probably harmless and should appreciate what seemed like good neighbor sentiment.

Retiring the broom, Terry went inside the house and settled in as best he could for his first night in a new place.

As soon as he sat down, the doorbell rang. It was a delivery of a big bouquet of roses from Teresa. A note was attached: "Roberto sends his best regards. He knew you would appreciate roses since 80 percent of cut roses come from Peru and Ecuador."

In the days that followed, Terry stayed busy settling into his house. He had sent Roberto several messages but hadn't heard back, which he thought was unusual. *That's not like Roberto. Perhaps he is in Chile visiting family.*

One of the first things Terry did was to set up a little office in his den where he could prepare for his upcoming classes. While getting his internet installed, he noticed a bundle of different cables in the closet that weren't connected to anything. He couldn't imagine what the previous owner would have used such robust wiring for. He pushed the wires aside to make room for some boxes.

Already a little homesick for his patio in Lima, Terry wanted to find a spot by his front door to plant a small rose garden like the one he had nurtured in Peru. He worked for several days preparing the bed, and every day at some point he would find Clint standing over him.

"Roses, eh? What kind? You know, they need to be hardy stock to survive our winters." Clint would just stand and watch for a few minutes, making Terry feel a bit uncomfortable.

"You seem to know a lot about roses and gardening, Clint."

"I'm a retired biology teacher. You can ask me most anything about plants." Not giving Terry a chance to ask any questions, Clint turned and walked back to his house. The smell of his pipe smoke lingered in the humid air.

The den, in which Terry spent much of his time, had a window facing the street. He began to notice that almost every day Clint would slowly walk down the street, pulling a little red wagon filled with an assortment of buckets, bottles, and tools.

After a week of watching Clint parade by the house, Terry decided to follow him.

Keeping a safe distance so as not to be noticed, he followed him for two blocks to the end of the street, where there was a heavily wooded area and a narrow dirt path. Clint disappeared into the woods. Terry followed the dirt path until he encountered a tall chain-link fence with razor wire at the top. Several "No Trespassing" signs were hung by a padlocked gate, but there was no sign of Clint. Through the trees in the distance, Terry could see what looked to be a small structure. He could also hear cadets doing their marching drills on the naval base.

Puzzled, Terry walked back to his house. On his way back, he felt the silence and solitude of his neighborhood. While houses lined the street, there was rarely anyone outside. As he approached his house, he saw a man putting a For Rent sign next door in front of Kenji's house.

"Did the family move out?" Terry asked.

"Yep, left in a hurry. That's the military for you."

A bit disappointed that his new neighborhood was changing already, Terry felt a bit sorry for Kenji and his family for having been uprooted so suddenly.

The next day from the den window, Terry saw Clint returning from the end of the street, pulling his wagon of unidentifiable paraphernalia. This time he got up and ran out the door to intercept him.

"Hey, Clint. How you doing? I've noticed you going by every day and was just curious what project you've got going on?" Terry usually wasn't this bold, but his curiosity had finally gotten to him.

Clint paused and puffed on his pipe, appearing unsure of how to respond. "There's a small native plant preserve adjacent to the base that I volunteer to take care of."

Terry was going to ask him about the protective fencing but didn't want to give away that he previously had followed him. Acting innocent, he commented, "Oh, that must be an interesting project. Is the woods open to the public?"

Clint looked at Terry without saying anything. After several uncomfortable moments of silence, Clint took the pipe out of his mouth and responded as he resumed his walk, "Not really. Navy property. Better admired from a distance."

Perplexed, but wanting to avoid any confrontation, Terry said, "Oh, I see," and walked back to the house. *How very strange,* he mused.

A week later while working in his garden, Terry was again startled once he looked up and saw Clint standing over him.

"Good morning, Clint." Terry continued working.

Clint carefully inspected his new garden. "I see all your roses are planted. Hope you mulched good."

Terry responded, "Say, Clint, I think I have a patch of poison ivy out back. Any suggestions how to get rid of it?"

Clint replied, "Wait here. I'll be right back."

About ten minutes later, Clint returned with a nondescript spray bottle filled with red liquid. "Here, spray this on it. But wear gloves. It can burn your skin and will kill anything you spray it on."

"Wow," Terry exclaimed, "some powerful stuff. Where do you buy it?"

"Can't buy it. Just be careful with it." Clint walked off.

While a neighborly gesture, this just seemed to add more mystery to the offbeat personality of Clint, who seemed to regularly appear out of nowhere. Terry ventured a guess that the red liquid may have been the cause of Clint's burned hands.

Terry was still adjusting to his new neighborhood. He had been so busy that he had ignored the vase of roses that Teresa had given him as a housewarming gift. They were dried up and unrecognizable. He took the vase to the kitchen and grabbed the roses to put them in the trash. He heard something fall on the floor. Looking around carefully at his feet, he saw a tiny black object. He picked it up and gasped. It was a tiny microphone.

"What the hell? Am I being bugged?" He stood frozen for a few seconds.

Then, in a panic, he dashed from room to room looking for cameras or other concealed devices. Finding nothing, he remembered the cables in the closet. He moved the boxes and could see that the cables entered the wall, but he couldn't figure out where they went. There wasn't a room on the other side of the closet. With his flashlight, he noticed a trapdoor in the floor. He carefully lifted it up, revealing a stairway down to a basement. With his heart pounding, he carefully went down the stairs. It was dark, but he saw a number of blinking lights. Above him was a string hanging from a ceiling light. He pulled it and couldn't believe what he saw. It appeared to be a high-tech communications, or comms, room full of computer screens and control panels.

He sat down to compose himself, then called Teresa.

The recorded voice answered, "This number is no longer in service."

Terry exclaimed, "What the hell!"

He searched the internet for Teresa's real estate firm but could not find it.

Totally exasperated, he opened a beer. "I need to get a hold of Roberto as soon as possible."

Roberto still hadn't returned his emails, so Terry decided to call the Peace Corps office in Lima. They were closed, but he left an urgent message for Roberto to call him. He logged on to his laptop and started composing a more detailed email to him, when the doorbell rang.

He peered through a side window and saw a puff of smoke, and figured it was Clint.

Terry opened the front door. "Hey, Clint. What's up?" Terry was still shaking from the shock of his recent discovery.

"Ah, just wondering if you want to come down to the little farm with me."

He wasn't sure he could take any more mystery at that moment. "What do you mean, 'little farm'?"

Clint answered, "You know, in the woods down the street. I noticed you followed me there the other day."

Terry, embarrassed that Clint had noticed he had followed him, was also surprised by Clint's sudden candor. He seemed like an entirely different person, more sociable and friendly.

Terry responded, "Well, uh, yeah, sure. Right now?"

"Yep, right now." Clint smiled for the first time.

The idea of getting away from his bugged house for a while made Terry happy. He responded, "Definitely, let's go!" He could send Roberto his distress email later, when he got back. Besides, he was curious what was behind the razor wire fence.

As Terry followed Clint to the fenced area at the end of the street, he asked him, "I'm curious; why are you showing me this now? I thought it was private."

Clint kept walking and said nothing. Terry shrugged his shoulders and followed.

When they arrived at the gate, Clint unlocked the padlock and opened the gate just wide enough for them to pass. He quickly closed it and secured it with the padlock.

It was a several-minutes' walk down the wooded path to another fence and gate, which secured a small shed and greenhouse. It was a quiet and beautiful setting, with wildflowers and flowering shrubs on either side of the path. Once again, Clint opened the gate and secured it after they had entered. The shed and greenhouse were partially obscured by wisteria vines, which had enveloped one entire side and the roof of the shed.

"Follow me," Clint ordered. He led Terry into the greenhouse.

Terry was stunned when they entered the seemingly run-down greenhouse. They passed rows of roses of all different sizes and colors. The fragrances were overwhelming, varying from sweet to spicy as they walked the length of the greenhouse. On a bench surrounded by miscellaneous tools and bottles of who-knows-what was the object of Clint's tour. It was a rose covered in crimson blooms with pink centers. The fragrance was of cinnamon and nutmeg.

"What a beautiful rose," Terry declared. Clint nodded in agreement. "So why are you showing me this? What are you doing here?" Terry's curiosity was evident.

"You'll know more when the time is right, but for now just know that I cultivate roses for different purposes—and for a very powerful organization. This rose has been the object of my work for the past seven years, but—"

Terry didn't let Clint finish. "What do you mean, when the time is right?"

"Terry, I rarely show this place to anyone. In fact, I'm not supposed to. But my work here is about done, and we both share an appreciation for roses. I thought if I'd share it with anyone, it should be you."

"I still don't understand why all the security," Clint said with a puzzled look.

Clint interrupted, saying, "Please don't ask any more questions. You're smart, loyal, and well-intentioned. Let's leave it at that for now."

Completely mystified by what he had just seen and heard, Terry dutifully followed Clint outside and back down the path toward their neighborhood. He tried one more time to question Clint, but Clint just turned around, smiled, and continued walking. When they arrived in front of Terry's house, Clint stopped and turned to him.

"Terry, I wish you success at the college. They are lucky to have you." Clint walked off, leaving Terry confused, concerned, and anxious, only to remember that he had an important email to send to Roberto.

Terry grabbed a beer and continued to compose the email to Roberto, asking for an explanation of all the mysteries surrounding his recent arrival: his apparent surveillance, the basement comms room, Teresa's disappearance, and Clint's secret project. Terry found himself getting angry as he was writing, but he wanted to remain respectful to Roberto, whom he still considered his best friend. Once finished, he hit send and went outside to check on his rose garden.

His young roses were still adjusting to having been transplanted. Blossoms were sparse. It made him reflect on how he was struggling to adapt to his new surroundings as well.

As he was finishing dinner that night, there was a knock on the door.

Terry hesitated to answer at first. He had been feeling anxious given everything that had transpired that day.

The knock was persistent. He opened the door.

It was Roberto.

"Roberto!" Terry exclaimed. His emotions varied from relief to anger. "What the—" he started to ask.

"May I come in?" Roberto asked as Terry remained frozen at the doorway.

"Uh, of course," Terry said, still shaking his head in amazement.

"Terry, I'm so sorry. I apologize for everything that's happened."

"What the hell is going on?" Terry went to the kitchen and brought back two beers. "I have a feeling we're going to need these."

Roberto said, "Let me start from the beginning." He took several large gulps of his beer. "I need to confess. I'm an operative for the Company—you know, the agency, the CIA. I have been for a long time. My Peace Corps work has been my official cover."

"Huh?" Terry shook his head. "Damn, like father, like son!" Terry said, recalling Roberto's father was a CIA operative in Chile.

Roberto continued, "As you know, the Chinese were trying to convince the Peruvian government to give them favored status for our ecotourism project, primarily as a way to gain influence in other government matters, such as access to natural resources and sway over border issues with Ecuador. We knew there was a mole in our Peace Corps office, and given your access to senior government officials, the agency had to be sure that you hadn't been compromised."

Terry stood up and argued, "Roberto, but you know me. I wouldn't—"

"Terry, sit down. I know. I know this is hard to take in. I didn't want to do this, but the agency made me. Remember, I tried to give you a subtle warning the night before you left about the 'ghosts.' You're my best friend, and I had faith in you, but the agency needed confirmation. I really feel bad—"

Terry interrupted. "Oh yeah, that bit about 'You can leave the mission, but the mission never leaves you.' Hmm."

"It had to be done to prove me right," Roberto confessed.

"So what about Teresa and the surveillance? What the hell is this place, this neighborhood, this house with a hidden comms room?" Terry's foot was tapping on the floor as he spoke.

Roberto continued, "Teresa is with the agency too. She manages the neighborhood."

"Manages the neighborhood?" Terry repeated.

"Yes, she controls who lives here." He took another long

sip of his beer and continued, "Terry, this was my house. I used to live here. Being located adjacent to the naval base, this neighborhood has advantages for the agency. Most people who live here are or were operatives like me. Each house has a similar comms room."

Terry asked, "And what if I had told Teresa that I didn't want to buy this house?"

Roberto answered, "She would have made you an offer you couldn't refuse."

"Oh, so you're the godfather now," Terry responded sarcastically. "Man, I don't believe this is happening. But it explains a lot." He continued, "And I suppose my job at Forest College was arranged too?"

Roberto paused. "Well—"

"Oh my God! The agency has taken total control of my life." Terry put his hand on his forehead. "What about the old man Clint next door and his secret workplace in the woods? He took me there today and said I'd understand eventually. Is today 'eventually'?"

Roberto answered, "Well, Clint is not really his name."

Terry interrupted, saying sarcastically, "Of course it's not."

Roberto continued, "He's a botanist working with the agency and who has been trying to hybridize a rose that will produce a rose hip containing a hallucinogenic compound to be used in interrogations. If successful, it would have been secretly mass-produced in the shadow of the rose trade of Peru and Ecuador. His experiments failed to yield the result desired."

Terry asked, "So why did Clint, or whatever his name

really is, finally feel comfortable about sharing this with someone like me?"

"Well, you're not just anyone, Terry," Roberto added with hesitancy in his voice.

"And what the hell does that mean?" Terry went to the kitchen to get another beer.

"Terry, I know you may not be able to forgive me for all of this. First, please know that as far as I'm concerned, nothing has changed between us. You're still my best friend. I know I have to earn your trust back. But first I have something else to tell you."

Terry sipped on his beer. "OK, what more can there be?"

"The agency wants you to continue the work Clint has started—"

Terry's heart skipped a beat. "Oh, hell no!"

"No, wait, let me explain. They abandoned that original idea and want to use your graduate work in botany for much more peaceful purposes. They're hoping you can create a hybrid rose that produces a compound in rose hips that can help treat victims of poison gas. It's a good project. It would help a lot of people." Roberto waited for a reaction.

Terry didn't wait to react. "Me? Let me stop you there. I have no intention to work for the CIA." After a pause, he asked, "Or don't I have a choice? Can I decline?"

"Sure, you can decline, but I'd have to kill you." Roberto laughed nervously. "Too soon?" His attempt to break the tension did bring a smile to Terry's face.

"Roberto, right now, especially with all that's happened recently, I think I'm better off remaining a civilian."

Roberto replied, "Listen, I totally understand how you're feeling right now. Just give it some thought. But you're absolutely the right person for this project, and I know you'd feel good about working on something that could save lives. And you still get to teach at the college."

Terry replied, "Roberto, I'm disappointed how all of this has gone down. While I have to admit there is something exciting about starting a new adventure, it's hard for me to imagine myself an operative of the CIA, even if it were for a good cause." After a pause, he asked, "So, my official cover would be teaching at the college?"

Roberto replied, "Yes, if that's OK with you. Please, just give it some serious thought."

"OK, but if I say no, do I have to sell the house and move?" A little frown came across Terry's face.

"Let's not worry about any of that right now. Maybe we'll laugh about this in our old age," Roberto joked. "Oh, and there's one more thing."

Terry groaned, saying, "Oh no."

Roberto opened the front door and brought in a large potted rose.

"Oh my God, that's Clint's rose," Terry proclaimed.

"Yes, he wanted you to have it."

"Wow, I have to call and thank him."

"Sorry, Terry, it's too late. Clint and his 'wife' were moved out last night."

Terry asked, "Moved out?"

"They're no longer with the agency. We all have our expiration dates." Roberto's smile left his face as soon as he said that.

Terry started to ask, "So what happens to—"

Roberto interrupted, "Don't ask, Terry. The agency loves

you when they're getting what they want. After that, you're expendable. But we all know that from the beginning."

Terry pressed Roberto on the expiration date comment. "Just tell me, are they killed, or given new identities as in witness protection?"

Roberto tried to ease Terry's concern. "Terry, you've watched too many spy movies. They just go back to a version of civilian life. It's a little more complicated for international espionage work, but you're not there yet."

Terry yelled, "Yet?"

"Just kidding again. Calm down, Che." Roberto gave Terry a hug and said he had to leave, explaining that he was being relocated from Peru but didn't know to where. He promised Terry he would stay in touch.

In subsequent weeks, Roberto sent Terry emails on a regular basis, although he never brought up the agency's request for him to continue Clint's work.

Terry planted Clint's rose among the other roses in his garden. It had one large crimson bloom.

After the drama with Roberto, Terry looked at all his neighbors with suspicion, wondering who they really were and what they were really up to.

* * *

The bell rang. Terry's class had just ended for the day and the last of the students had gone. While clearing his desk to go home, he noticed someone sitting in the shadows at the back of the classroom. The man was dressed in a black suit and wore dark sunglasses. A ponytail protruded from beneath his fedora.

Approaching with caution, Terry asked, "Can I help you?"

The man stood up and, from underneath his coat, pulled out a crimson rose. In a whiny, sniveling voice, he inquired, "Can you tell me the story about this rose?"

Terry woke up in a sweat. It wasn't the first weird dream he had had since returning. He put on his robe and walked out the front door of his house to check on his roses. With a sigh of relief, he saw that Clint's rosebush was safe. It still had its one crimson bloom intact.

A couple of days later, Terry noticed a brown envelope leaning against his front door. He brought it in the house and opened it. Inside was a set of keys and a cryptic note:

> Keys to greenhouse gate. Instructions will follow about project and official cover status. Basement comms room back online.
>
> —Che

Terry was surprised how calm he was. He thought, *That slickster. Maybe he's right … the mission will never leave me.*

He walked out the front door to his rose garden. Gently cupping the crimson rose blossom in his hand, he whispered, "Undercover rose, indeed."

QUIXOTIC IN QUITO

*P*AINTED LIKE A GIANT MULTICOLORED parrot, the Ecuatoriana jet had just landed in Ecuador at Quito's Mariscal Sucre International Airport. On board the flight was Cliff, a young American ready to begin a yearlong consulting mission for the United Nations. It wasn't the first time Cliff had lived abroad. He was excited but knew it would be a challenging experience working a full-time job conducted entirely in Spanish.

Because there were several unplanned diversions due to weather, it had been an exhausting flight of nearly twenty-four hours from Los Angeles. Cliff's anxious anticipation of what lay ahead and the long flight had left him drained. He felt disheveled and knew he was wearing a heavy five-o'clock shadow. The airport seemed quiet and uncongested as the plane taxied up to the terminal.

Cliff lined up with the rest of the passengers to disembark. As he descended the stairs that had been wheeled up to the plane's doorway, he noticed several people in suits gathered at the bottom but was too tired to give it much thought. When he reached the bottom of the stairway, he turned to follow the other equally exhausted passengers to the terminal.

Suddenly, someone shouted, "Señor Cliff Logan?" Cliff continued walking, focused only on getting to the terminal to retrieve his luggage. The person shouted again and ran up from behind to gently tap him on the shoulder. Cliff turned around, thinking he must have dropped something. Standing in front of him with a bright wide smile was a strikingly handsome man with short black hair and a thin mustache.

Extending his arm to Cliff, the sharply dressed gentleman said, "Mr. Logan, I'm Marco Antonio, the director of UN operations for South America. Welcome to Quito."

Not having expected to see anyone until the next day, Cliff was slow to respond and had to suddenly switch his language gears from English to Spanish.

"Oh." He paused awkwardly. "It's a pleasure to meet you, Director. I'm looking forward to working on the project here."

"Please, we are informal here. Call me Marco," the director replied.

As they continued their conversation, a man with a large camera began taking photographs. He asked Marco and Cliff to pose together.

Marco explained, "Having UN workers in Quito is a big deal for the local government. We are lucky to be welcomed guests here in Ecuador, which is not always the case in South America."

Cliff was self-conscious about how unkempt he must have looked, and at the same time he tried not to embarrass himself by staring at Marco Antonio's handsome gaze. He responded, "That's very comforting to hear. My email from your office instructed me to go to the regional headquarters at nine o'clock tomorrow morning for orientation. Is that correct?"

"Yes. We'll have a continental breakfast prepared, and you will be joined by two other consultants, who will be on your team. I know you must be tired from your long trip, so we'll let you get some rest. There will be a car waiting for you at baggage claim to take you to your hotel." With both hands, Marco grabbed Cliff's arm. "Until tomorrow."

Cliff was eager to get to his hotel room so he could shower and eat an early dinner. He needed a good night's sleep before meeting his UN team early in the morning.

More clearheaded after his shower and dinner, Cliff was finally hit with the thought that his adventure had finally begun. He replayed in his mind the memorable greeting he had received from Director Antonio at the airport.

Cliff understood that most of the LGBTQ community in Ecuador was underground and not publically accepted. A social life would be nice but wasn't a priority. His friends back home would always kid him that he lived his life "inside a romance novel." His response was that the real world hadn't been able to give him what he was looking for—a sweet romantic adventure.

At his going away party the week before, he joked, "I'm headed to South America to find my Don Quixote, or at least a handsome Latin knight."

One friend yelled out, "OK, Dulcinea. Good luck with that!"

Cliff laughed. "Well, maybe a gay Sancho Panza."

The next morning Cliff woke up early, still jet-lagged but eager to meet his colleagues. He stopped in the hotel coffee shop for a quick cup of coffee and glanced at the complimentary copy of the local newspaper, *El Comercio*. "Oh my gosh!" he exclaimed out loud, which caused a couple sitting nearby to turn their heads. "That's me and Marco on the front page!"

He read the short caption underneath the photo: "United Nations director Marco Antonio welcomes new team member, Cliff Logan, from America."

"Damn, I look like hell," he mumbled quietly. Looking at Marco standing next to him in the photo, he thought, *He is even more handsome than I remember.*

Noticing that the couple was still looking his way, Cliff quickly folded up the paper and walked the short distance to the UN regional office. By the time he arrived at the office he was huffing and puffing, forgetting that Quito was situated at ten thousand feet at the foot of the Pichincha volcano.

He entered a small conference room, where he was greeted by Marco and a number of UN staff. An older man with thinning white hair was introduced as his team leader and a rather dowdy middle-aged woman as his project partner. They were both from Chile.

While Cliff's teammates were introducing themselves, he couldn't help but be distracted by the strikingly handsome director, Marco. Marco's tailored slacks revealed his narrow waist, and the fitted shirt pronounced his broad shoulders and well-developed arms. He was heavily bearded but shaven except for the mustache. He had a caramel complexion, and his broad smile resulted in a slight squinting of his eyes, which Cliff found sexy.

"Again, Cliff, welcome. I hope to see more of you." Marco made direct eye contact with Cliff and grabbed his arm with both hands as he had done at the airport

Cliff's first week was spent getting to know his team and becoming familiar with the proposed project.

Weeks passed. Work was going smoothly, but he hadn't seen Marco since the first day. His teammates said that Marco was from Brazil, was married, and traveled much of the time. He rented a home in Quito, but he and his wife lived permanently in Bahia, Brazil.

In subsequent weeks, Marco made several trips to visit the team. He usually was dressed in casual attire—slacks and a shirt with the top buttons undone, revealing a tanned and hairy chest.

"I hear things are going well, Cliff. Have you adjusted to life in Quito?" Marco leaned over Cliff's shoulder from behind, leaving Cliff in an invisible cloud of his manly but sweet scent.

"Yes, Director—I mean, Marco. I love Quito. I found a nice apartment in the Amazonas area of town."

"Ah, that's a great area—a lot of good restaurants and nightlife." Marco gave Cliff a wink.

Not knowing how to respond, Cliff said, "Yes, the people have all been very nice and welcoming."

Without hesitation, Marco added, "Well, while I'm in town, please don't hesitate to call if you need anything. We should have dinner sometime. And I can take you to some spots known mostly to locals only." He patted Cliff on the shoulder and walked away.

During other visits, Marco made the same general invitation but never really followed through. Cliff was disappointed but also a bit relieved as he didn't want to add any tension to his work relationships. His teammates never mentioned receiving similar invitations, although Marco would occasionally take them all out to lunch.

Months later, Marco had a pool party and barbecue at his house for everyone. His wife was visiting from Brazil. Dressed in a tank top and swim trunks, Marco showed his true Latin spirit in encouraging everyone to dance, swim, and drink.

"Cliff, can I make you another margarita?" he asked with his naked arm wrapped around him.

Cliff responded, "Yes, but this should be the last. I'm really starting to feel them."

"Good, that's the whole point!" Marco laughed and was clearly feeling his drinks as well.

Cliff hadn't seen Marco in that way before, uninhibited and physical, yet still keeping respectable boundaries.

Cliff had learned from past trips to Brazil that, in general, Brazilians were more physically and socially engaging than neighboring populations. He didn't suspect that Marco had any intentions other than to be his cheerful self.

To compensate for lack of an actual social life, Cliff would occasionally fantasize about him, his Don Marco Quixote. Pictures of Marco were always present on their website with updates on his travels and meetings. Cliff checked the website every few days to see if there were any new photos.

Occasionally, Marco would email him a photo from some exotic location and relate a story about a great party or dinner. Cliff was surprised at Marco's indifference to his own personal privacy. Cliff didn't share the email updates with his teammates. He suspected that they hadn't received similar messages after they complained they rarely heard from the director unless he needed some information about the project. While this made Cliff feel special, it also made him wonder why he was getting privileged treatment. He wanted to ask Marco but knew this would be crossing a boundary, which might create tension between them.

Months passed with the same routine, until one evening Cliff heard a loud knock on his apartment door. "Who's there?" he asked, not accustomed to visitors.

There was a pause, and then a muffled voice said, "It's Marco."

With his jaw dropped open, Cliff thought, *Marco is here?* He opened the door. Marco seemed embarrassed but asked, "May I come in, my friend?"

"Of course, Marco. Is everything OK?"

Marco appeared distraught. From his strong breath, it was obvious he had been drinking.

"Please, sit on the couch. Can I get you some water or anything?" Cliff asked nervously.

"Yes, that would be nice. And I'm so sorry to bother you, Cliff. I find this very embarrassing, but I felt more comfortable coming to you."

Cliff's head was spinning. He couldn't imagine what might have happened. Not knowing what to say, he sat next to Marco on the couch and asked, "Sure, just let me know how I can help."

"Cliff, I just need a place to stay tonight and get cleaned up. I need to be discreet, and staying at a hotel would raise too many questions." Marco drank some water and rested his head in his hands.

After a few minutes, he explained that his wife had learned that he'd had an affair. They had argued, and she told him to leave. He admitted he had done this before, which she ignored, but this time it was with someone she knew.

"I know it wasn't right. I feel ashamed." Marco looked as if he wanted to cry, but he struggled to maintain his composure.

Pouring a glass of wine for both of them, mainly to calm his own nerves, Cliff said, "I'm sorry, I just don't know what to say. But you're more than welcome to stay tonight."

"Thanks, Cliff. I won't forget your kindness."

Exhausted, Marco started to fall asleep on the sofa and fell over onto Cliff's lap. Cliff looked down at handsome Marco, wondering if he was dreaming all of this. Despite enjoying the moment, he knew he had to get Marco stretched out on the couch. Cliff felt his guest's hairy legs as he lifted Marco on the couch. He grabbed his muscular shoulders and arms to maneuver him so he could sleep. He covered him with a blanket, turned out the lights, and went to his own bedroom.

Cliff got very little sleep that night. He thought to himself, *Marco never mentioned if it was a man or woman with whom he'd had the affair.* While Cliff was no prude, he did respect boundaries. As attractive as Marco was, Cliff had learned from a mistake he made years earlier not to cross the boss–subordinate line with personal involvement, and that married men were taboo—also a lesson learned the hard way.

Morning came very early for both men.

Cliff noticed Marco was very quiet. He thought, *Probably still embarrassed and a little hungover.*

"I put out some fresh towels for you, Marco. Hopefully, you'll feel a little better after a shower. And I left a clean shirt for you hanging in the bathroom." Cliff had picked out one of his best shirts.

Marco showered and got dressed. Returning to the common area, he said, "Cliff, I'm forever grateful to you and will never forget your kindness. And I know you'll be discreet about this."

"Of course," Cliff responded.

Both men stood, face-to-face. Marco began to lean forward. For a moment Cliff thought something was going to happen. But Marco suddenly pulled back and hurriedly walked out the door.

A few days later a package arrived at the office for Cliff. He didn't open it until he was alone. It was the shirt he had lent Marco. It had been laundered, but Cliff decided never to wear that shirt again. He kept it in his closet as a way of being close to a man he had fantasized about for so many months.

Marco never talked about the incident. He remained friendly with Cliff, but instead of the customary emails, he would send him little gifts from places he had been. They usually had notes attached, ending with the salutation, "For my loyal friend—always."

The year passed quickly, and Cliff's contract in Quito was ending. As was tradition, the regional office held a going away dinner. While everyone was drinking their cocktails, Cliff quietly revisited the past year in his mind. He felt proud about his contributions to the project. Everyone wished him well except for one person: Marco. He didn't attend. Initially, Cliff felt a bit hurt but later thought maybe it was better that way. Marco's nighttime knock on his door months earlier was still fresh in his mind.

The next evening Cliff headed to the airport for the flight to UN headquarters in New York, where he was to begin an administrative position. He broke his promise about never wearing that special shirt again. Instead, he decided it would bring him comfort on the long flight.

As he got in line to board the plane, he heard someone yell, "Mi querido Cliff!"

To the surprise of others in line, Marco pushed through the crowd and gave Cliff a long-lasting embrace.

"I didn't come to say goodbye. Since you're still with the UN, I'll always be able to find you. Have a safe flight, my friend." He gave Cliff a kiss on each cheek.

Cliff was lost for words as Marco's hazel eyes pierced him like a laser beam. Marco looked as impressively handsome as he had when he greeted him that first day at the airport.

He handed Cliff an envelope and put his finger to his mouth, indicating nothing needed to be said. He disappeared into the crowd as quickly as he had appeared.

Shortly after takeoff, Cliff drank some liquid courage before opening Marco's envelope. Inside was a newspaper clipping of the photo taken the day of his arrival in Quito. Across the photo Marco had written the following:

The time isn't always right.

With much affection,
Marco

Having quickly downed his glass of wine, Cliff asked the flight attendant for another bottle. He stared out the window and watched the snow-covered Cotopaxi volcano slowly fade in the distance. His eyes got moist.

With the photo still in his hand, he wondered if Marco really had romantic expectations. Perhaps they both were surprised to have found themselves on their own quixotic pursuits with one another. But unlike Don Quixote, maybe they didn't depart totally defeated. Instead, in some distant way, Cliff thought that maybe they would remain one another's knight-errant, destined to cross paths once more.

Then Cliff shook his head and thought, *Nah, at least it was a good fantasy.*

He put the photo in his wallet and figured that his friends were right—true romance was only found in cheesy novels. Still, he felt warm and comforted by Marco's surprise appearance, and soon fell asleep.

Four months had passed. Cliff had received several emails from Marco during that time. They were short notes just to say hello and to wish him well in his New York post. Cliff would respond in kind.

It was just before the holiday season, and Cliff had been invited to attend a UNICEF fundraiser in New York. He had just entered the hotel ballroom when he ran into one of his former teammates from Quito. They chatted briefly, and his colleague said, "We heard Director Marco got a divorce."

Cliff replied, "I'm not surprised." His colleague gave him a puzzled look, but the formal dinner was going to start soon, so Cliff excused himself to go to his assigned table.

No one was seated yet. He walked around the table to look for his name tag and suddenly stopped. Next to his assigned seat was a name tag that read, "Director Marco Antonio."

Cliff thought, *Now, is that just coincidence or what?*

Suddenly from behind, he felt a tap on his shoulder. Cliff excitedly stood up and turned around. "Marco, it's good … uh … oh … Hello, Cap, it's you. How are you doing?"

"Cap" was short for Nick Capolitano, Cliff's boss in the New York office.

"You OK, Cliff? You look disappointed." Cap chuckled.

Clearly embarrassed, Cliff recovered. "Oh, I'm fine. I really appreciate you inviting me to this event. You know how much I like the UNICEF organization."

Cap responded, "I know, Cliff. That's why I've asked our new UNICEF director to contact you to see how you can get more involved."

"Thanks, Cap. I appreciate that!"

"Well, listen, I have to go to my table. Enjoy the evening."

After dinner had ended, several short speeches followed. During the course of the evening, Cliff had glanced several times with disappointment at the empty chair next to him.

The last speaker completed his final remarks and said, "Excuse me, everyone. We have a special announcement to make. We were hoping he would make it in time for our dinner, but he just arrived from a late flight from Brazil. Let me introduce the new director of UNICEF, Marco Antonio."

Cliff knocked over his water glass. He noticed Marco looking in his direction from the stage. Neither of them were able to conceal their widening smiles.

DOGGONE

HE LOUD CLAP OF THUNDER scared Nona. The six-year-old yellow Lab jumped up on to Avery's lap. She had never gotten over her fear of thunderstorms, but Avery, a retired fireman, was always there to comfort her. He had recently adopted Nona from the Pine Woods Dog Shelter, which was owned by his friend Sherry.

Avery was a widower and had lived alone for many years. He found his only joy in the company of his dogs. Prior to adopting Nona, he had a chocolate Lab named Hershey, whom he also had adopted from the Pine Woods shelter. Hershey was an eight-year-old rescue who had advanced kidney disease. With the dog given up for nearly dead, Avery, after adopting him, and after months of home-based care, slowly nursed Hershey back to an acceptable quality of life in a loving home. The vet thought it was nothing short of a miracle. Avery remembered the glimmer of hope in Hershey's eyes the first day he saw him, when he just knew he had to provide him a home where he could live the rest of his life with some dignity. Hershey would often spend days at the firehouse with Avery before he retired. Hershey was eleven when he lost his battle with the disease.

One day, Avery took a few pictures of Nona while she was playing in the backyard. She seemed to be unusually full of spirit, rolling around, jumping, and barking. He wanted a photo of her that he could frame and display next to the one of his devoted Hershey. Avery had no other family, and the photo of Hershey was the only one in his house, prominently displayed on his fireplace mantel.

After their play session in the yard, Avery came back in to the house to make lunch. While his soup was heating, he grabbed his phone to look at the photos he had just taken of Nona.

"What the—!"

After almost knocking the pot of soup off the stove, Avery went to the kitchen table and sat down. Trying to hold the phone steady despite his heavy breathing, he looked closely at the photos he had just taken. Behind Nona was a faint image of another dog sitting upright, head facing forward. Avery removed his glasses and wiped them off, thinking there must be dirt on the lenses.

How can this be? he thought. *That's Hershey!*

He looked at several other photos he had taken, and they all had a faint black-and-white image of Hershey sitting behind Nona.

At first Avery kept this to himself as he didn't want anyone to think he was crazy. For months whenever he took of picture of Nona, an image of Hershey would appear behind her. There were times late at night when he heard two dogs playing in the living room. At first it was a bit unnerving, but after a while the sound became comforting.

Often, he would find some of Hershey's old toys in Nona's dog bed.

He often muttered out loud to himself, "I'm old, and maybe a bit crazy and delusional, but that's OK—the world out there is probably a lot crazier than me."

He confided in his best friend, Sherry Leonard, the owner of the Pine Woods Dog Shelter. She would smile and tell him, "Oh, Avery, those dogs are just working their magic on you. You're not crazy. And I've told you before that all my dogs here are special!"

Nona's death came a few years later. Avery would often sit in his easy chair and stare at the photos of Hershey and Nona on the fireplace mantel. He had debated whether to adopt another dog, but his own health was failing and he didn't think he could provide adequate care for another companion.

Avery passed away soon after Nona's death. With no immediate family, he had named Sherry the executrix of his small estate. He left instructions that he wanted to be cremated and his ashes scattered in the woods not far from his home. He was specific that they be placed underneath a small footbridge that spanned a tiny creek. Hershey loved this spot during his walks, and even Nona would tug at the leash to go under the bridge when they passed. He also had asked that the ashes of both Hershey and Nona be scattered with his.

Sherry followed through with Avery's wish regarding his remains, but after looking through every drawer and cupboard in his house, she could not find any trace of the dogs' ashes.

Later that year, Avery's home was sold to a young couple, Bill and Sally, who fell in love with the quaint little house and the nice backyard. They had a young golden retriever named Ed. Having just moved in, they were still unpacking and Sally was cleaning a closet in one of the bedrooms. As she reached to clean an upper shelf, she saw something in the far corner. With a broom, she gently nudged it toward her. It was a very small wood box tied with twine. She brought it down to the kitchen.

"Bill, look what I found up in the closet."

Bill came in the kitchen and joked, "Well, let's open it. Maybe it's full of gold doubloons."

They cut off the twine and opened the box. Inside were two small plastic bags filled with a grayish powder. There was a small note that read as follows:

> Sherry, these are the ashes of Hershey and Nona. As instructed in my note to you, please scatter these with mine under the bridge in the woods.
>
> Thanks, and bless you.
>
> —Avery

Bill and Sally were disappointed that their treasure wasn't gold doubloons, but they were touched by the sentiment of the note. They had no idea who Sherry was, but they saw that the message was written on notepaper from the Pine Woods Dog Shelter.

Bill dialed the phone number for the shelter.

"Pine Woods Dog Shelter. How can I help you?"

"Hello, is there someone there named Sherry?" he inquired.

"Yes, this is Sherry."

Bill explained their discovery. Sherry exclaimed, "Oh

my God!" She explained she had been friends with the previous owner and that she had tried to comply with his wishes but couldn't find the dogs' ashes. "May I stop by your house later today and pick up the ashes? I really want to fulfill his final request."

Sherry went to the house to get the ashes, and both Bill and Sally asked if they could join her when she took the ashes to the woods. Sherry wasn't sure at first, but the couple explained that since it represented some history in their new house, they wanted to participate.

A few days later the three walked through the woods to the same place where Sherry had scattered Avery's ashes. She said, "I hope you guys keep this between us since it's probably not legal to do this." She explained how dedicated Avery was, not only to his dogs but also to the shelter. "Our dogs are special. They have a magical quality, and Avery learned to appreciate that."

The couple agreed. They thought Sherry's comment about her dogs' special "magical qualities" was hyperbole but didn't doubt her commitment to the shelter.

Some days later, Bill and Sally took Ed for a walk in the woods and noticed that when they came near the little footbridge, he got excited and started whimpering. They figured it was just coincidence.

A couple of weeks later they paid a visit to the animal shelter and told Sherry that they wanted to adopt a companion for Ed. They left that day with a yellow Lab named Tillie. It wasn't more than a week since their new pup had been home when Sally yelled from the patio, "Bill, you won't believe what just happened!" Little did they know that their magical journey was just beginning.

CRUSHING CONFESSIONS

*T*HEY SAY CUPID'S ARROW NEEDS to be sharp if it is to stick. As I look back on my romantic adventures, I find that it's easy to categorize them as successes, failures, or nonstarters. In retrospect, it's the nonstarters that hold a fascination for me—the crushes.

By definition, to crush on is to have a brief but intense infatuation for someone, usually someone unattainable and inappropriate, and often disappointing.

To the current generation, whose social lives revolve to a large degree around arm's-length social media apps, this view of crushes may appear as quaint and old-fashioned. Perhaps it is. But back in the "old days" of the 1970s and 1980s, it was difficult to wear your orientation on your sleeve, and there was no such thing as an internet safe space where a social media app could embolden an approaching stranger to acknowledge his or her attraction.

For me, the crush was the precursor of swiping right. I imagine most of us have had at least one or more crushes, and while most were probably no more than useless entanglements, they may have been instructional in the ways of romance.

This is where I begin.

"INNOCENT"—CURTIS

Curtis was my first real crush. We met one summer on the lake where our families had vacation cabins. We spent much of the summer waterskiing and swimming, usually meeting out on the water by his dock early each afternoon. His uncle had a nice boat that he let Curtis use as long as he didn't hotdog around. Curtis's chocolate Lab, Comet, was always by his side no matter where we went.

I was sixteen, and although Curtis was two years my junior, he seemed years ahead of me in his confidence, experience, and physical appearance. He had an exotic look—olive skin, dark hair, trim and fit body. His face was showing prebeard peach fuzz, which I envied. In subsequent summers that fuzz would darken and fill in. His dark eyebrows were like crowns above his green eyes. I found myself trying not to be obvious when I looked at him, especially when he would climb into the boat soaking wet, his skin glistening. I found his easygoing swagger both attractive and intimidating. He told me his father was from Brazil and his mother was Japanese. He was born when they were still teenagers, and his mother left soon afterward. He joked that he was a mistake, but I could only think to myself, *What a mistake!*

He said his father was busy with his landscaping business back in Illinois, so he'd been spending summers at his uncle's cabin.

At sixteen, I had little concept of being gay. I just knew that there were certain things about some men that I liked. My time with Curtis was innocent fun, and the summer passed quickly. At the end of that first summer, he came by on his last day to say goodbye and to add that he hoped to see me the next year. I suddenly realized I didn't know where he lived, so I hurriedly asked. He told me the name of a small town that I had never heard of. Later, my father said it was about seventy miles outside the city where we lived.

That fall, Curtis invited me to visit. My father agreed to drive and drop me off for a long weekend. The hour-and-a-half drive seemed to last forever. Following Curtis's directions, we turned off the main highway at an exit that had a sign: No Services This Exit. I thought, *How cool.* He and his father were roughing it in the middle of nowhere, adding to the mystique of my new friend. We drove up a long gravel driveway to a large log home. Parked off to the side were several large trucks lettered with Ribeira Landscaping on their sides. We were greeted first by Comet, the Lab, and then Curtis, who looked even older to me than he had that previous summer. Paulo, his father, introduced himself. He was an imposingly handsome man in his own right. I immediately saw from where Curtis had inherited his own good looks.

I traveled out for long weekends a couple of times that winter on Amtrak as one of the stops of the Southwest Chief heading west was not far from Curtis's town. His father was happy to pick me up at the station. I felt Curtis and I had become good friends, playing slot cars and hiking on his father's small farm. To the side of the house was a large pen with the half dozen goats Curtis was raising. Behind the house were endless rows of trees and shrubs that his father grew for sale.

Paulo was a very young father and easily engaged with us. After a brief discussion about Curtis's goats and his desire to be a veterinarian, Paulo asked me what I wanted to do after I graduated. I told him I liked plants and wanted to study botany when I went to college. I followed up with a lot of questions about what a landscaping business entailed. Impressed by all my questions, Paulo took Curtis and me with him on some of his landscaping jobs, initially to observe, but eventually we found ourselves carrying bags of manure and compost. I didn't mind as long as I was with Curtis. Paulo would refer to us jokingly as his junior partners. I grew very fond of Paulo too and thought Curtis was very lucky to have such a cool, hip dad.

We enjoyed one another's company for the next two summers. Each subsequent winter I found myself daydreaming about Curtis and the summer to come, hoping he was doing the same.

On the third summer, we again renewed our schedule of waterskiing each afternoon, but he seemed a bit more distant and distracted. He was less focused on me and kept talking about girls at his school and one in particular whom he thought was pretty. This didn't discourage my attraction toward him, but it did leave me a little disappointed that there was someone else interfering with our friendship. I still wasn't out at this point and didn't really understand why I was feeling this way. At the end of the summer I went to his uncle's house to say goodbye and was told Curtis had left the day before. I was crushed that he hadn't said goodbye.

Curtis and I spoke a couple of times that winter, but

I never received an invitation to his farm. The following summer I went by his dock. The boat was there, but it was covered with a tarp. Days passed and I finally got the nerve to knock on his uncle's door. The uncle told me Curtis wasn't coming up that summer. He winked and said he had a girlfriend and wanted to spend the summer at home. Curtis spoke a couple more times that winter but never got together again.

Several years had passed when I received a short letter from him saying he was engaged. By that time I was more self-aware and understood why I had been so attracted to Curtis. It was my first crush disappointment, but it wasn't going to be my last.

"UNATTAINABLE"—ALEJANDRO

I spent part of my junior year of college abroad at El Computense University of Madrid. I was on a tight budget and lived in one of three rooms rented out by an older woman who owned the apartment and lived there as well. She had strict rules for her tenants and cooked us limited meals that we ate in our rooms. One room was rented by another student, and the other room was vacant. One afternoon while I was studying, I heard a commotion in the hallway and poked my head out the door.

Graciela was our salty landlady and was normally a subdued and serious woman with a strict motherly demeanor. But that day she was excited and speaking so rapidly that I could hardly understand her. She appeared to be welcoming a new tenant, but I couldn't see much because the room was on the other side of the apartment past the kitchen.

Later that day, Graciela knocked on my door to give me the two oranges, which she rationed to her tenants each day. I asked her who the new tenant was. She said he was a young bullfighter from Mexico who had been invited to an exhibition fight in Spain. He was accompanied by his brother. She shared none of the enthusiasm with me that she had displayed earlier, and requested that I didn't bother him, implying he was a celebrity deserving of special treatment and privacy. I soon realized she considered him more important than her other tenants. The relatively lavish meals she provided him and his brother supported that theory.

Several days later, I had returned from class and saw the two Mexican guests standing in the kitchen eating snacks, something Graciela would have forbidden anyone else to do. Both guys were very young and good-looking, but immediately I could tell which one was the bullfighter. He indeed looked like a celebrity model and was much more neatly groomed than his brother. He sported a short black mustache, heavy beard stubble, and long sideburns. His black hair was thick but cut short. His shirt and pants clung tightly to his slim but solid frame.

His brother spoke first, in Spanish. "Hello, I'm Raul, and this is my brother Alejandro."

Alejandro nodded. Both had disarming smiles and deep voices. Nothing more was said that day, but I went back to my room with my head spinning at how stunning Alejandro was. I knew that some of my enthusiasm was because he was an actual bullfighter, even though I wasn't initially able to confirm this since there was no internet in the 1970s.

The following day was Saturday—no class, time to kill.

I was getting ready to go out and explore the city, when there was a knock on my door. Expecting Graciela with her daily delivery of oranges, I was pleasantly surprised to see Raul in his jeans and T-shirt. He asked if I wanted to go play pool with them. Of course, I said yes, knowing full well I would likely make a fool of myself since I had played pool only a couple of times in my life.

Alejandro was more talkative and animated that day. He laughed a lot, which showed off his bright toothy smile. Despite his dimples, he had a very macho demeanor. Occasionally, he would relax, seemingly letting his macho guard down. Then suddenly he would straighten up and say something in a deep voice as if to remind me that the bullfighter had not left the room. I thought that acting the role of a macho bullfighter must be exhausting, but I was enjoying every moment of it.

I asked why he was here. He proudly explained that he was famous in Mexico and wanted to earn similar fame in Spain. He wore a short-sleeve shirt unbuttoned halfway down. I was sure he intended to show off the forest of black hair on his chest. Occasionally, he would put his arm around me while making jokes. It was more a gesture of being in control than one of affection. It didn't matter as I had a bullfighter for a friend—at least for a few moments.

They asked where I was from. I said Chicago. They responded excitedly, assuming that my parents must be gangsters. When I said no, they seemed very disappointed.

When we returned to the apartment, I was surprised when Alejandro invited me to their room to show me his bullfighting outfit. At first, I wasn't sure whether to think of it more as a costume than formal dress, but as bullfighters are regarded as artists as well as athletes, I was sure his attire was as important to him as ballet shoes were to a ballerina. I was in awe as he put on his gold-adorned vest and hat. He didn't put on the tight pants, as that would have required a more complicated and private wardrobe change. The vest was beautifully adorned with gold beads and threads. It did have the appearance of a theater costume, that is, until he told me to try it on. I was surprised but honored.

As he lowered the vest and I put my arms through it, I could feel the tremendous weight of the garment, which was thick and heavily adorned. I soon realized that this was no theater outfit. Alejandro then went to the closet and retrieved his sword. As he handed it to me, the weight of its mighty blade almost took me to the ground. Both brothers laughed at me, and Alejandro sympathetically patted me on the back. I could feel his breath on my neck and smell his subtle scent. I returned to my room, ate my oranges, and let my swirling thoughts settle in on one long daydream.

Willing to endure the disapproving eye of Graciela, I purposely paused by the kitchen whenever I left or entered the apartment, hoping to catch a glimpse of Alejandro. But after a week's time, my matador crush had departed for good. I'd soon realize that not all things are as they appear. This was no more apparent to me than as you'll find in my next story.

"A LESSON LEARNED"—DAN

He was channeling Carol Channing while doing a faux striptease on the beach. He had little left to strip off but a skimpy Speedo. But I'll get back to that in a few moments.

I had just started to experience gay life—discos, parties, and yes, gay magazines. It was the mid-1970s and a new publication had just come out called *Playgirl*. It was supposed to be for women what *Playboy* was for men. I thought, *Finally, a more mainstream magazine that a gay man can enjoy too.* I was coming home from work and saw a new issue displayed at the local newsstand. The man on the cover caught my attention and checked all the boxes: dark complexion, black hair, heavy dark beard, and very fit.

I couldn't get home fast enough to open the magazine to the centerfold and read about his story. His name was Dan. I was captivated. His poses were natural, oozing of masculinity. Despite his exotic look, he sported a smile that made him seem approachable. The story line painted him as the sexy guy next door who could be working on his car or taking his girlfriend on a romantic date. I visited that issue often for more than a year. There were other issues with exotic men, but I always came back to Dan.

About a year later a friend asked me to go to Fire Island with him for a long weekend. Seeing as the place was legendary as a summer vacation mecca for the gay community, I couldn't turn down the invitation. His friends had rented a beach house for the summer, and we were welcome to stay as long as we helped with cooking and cleaning.

I was surprised and somewhat intimidated by the sheer number of attractive men on the island, all seemingly available at the cost of a few winks. One afternoon we gathered at one of the houses that was hosting a tea (cocktail) party. Most of the guys were shirtless, wearing Speedos or shorts, and the crowd was animated with laughter and loud conversation. We joined a small crowd that was cheering and yelling, "Take it off! Take it off!" (Now we return to the Carol Channing moment.)

My friend and I moved closer to the guy performing. I found myself right behind him. He had his back to me but was so close that I could smell the cocoa butter on his shoulders. He was flamboyant and very popular with the crowd, who gathered in numbers to watch his performance. For a moment, he lost his balance on the sand and backed in to me, leaving a sweat mark on my T-shirt. He turned around to say sorry. I was in shock. It was my fantasy dreamboat, Dan! I put my head on my friend's shoulder and whispered, "It's Dan."

While Dan was attractive, his flamboyant and campy demeanor was not the image portrayed in the magazine. I felt let down and deceived—crushed. There's something my friends called the "Monet experience." It's when you see someone from a distance or in a photo and you imagine them to look or be a certain way, but when you get up close, like a Monet painting, all the gritty details are revealed. The photos of Dan did accurately capture his good looks and athletic body, but he was a pint-sized version of the person I would have expected—a buff 5'4", perhaps, but not the 6'2" as claimed in the magazine. Nor was he the masculine hero I'd been led to fantasize about.

After Dan apologized, I confessed to him, "You know, I bought that magazine because of you, and looked at it often." I flashed an embarrassing smile.

"Oh, that rag!" He laughed. "I did that on a dare. At least it helped to pay for some of my tuition."

He explained he was a dentist but did drag and stripping for fun. It was clear that his biography in the magazine was pure fiction. He wasn't busy blowing the socks off women as described in his backstory; he wasn't a welder; and he didn't raise horses. His bio claimed he could suck the chocolate off a peanut—the one statement in the magazine I figured might be accurate.

Deflated and disappointed by the magazine's deceptive story, I did learn a valuable lesson, that is, not to judge. While Dan may have been the diva of the beach crowd, he also had an accomplished career.

While it took me months before I could open that issue again without its provoking a deep sigh, I looked at Dan much differently and was actually rather proud I had met him. I learned that our community is rich in its diversity.

Still, sometimes it's best not to meet your heroes.

As time passed, I also learned that crushes don't become any easier to accept.

"BRIEF"—FRANK

I met Frank at a friend's dinner party. He was on one-day shore leave from his Pacific Fleet ship in San Diego.

Handsome, warm, romantic—bold, black and beautiful—he sent photos from the ship for several months after they sailed … and sailed … and sailed.

Bye, Frank.

"ELECTRIFIED"—RUSSELL

For several months I worked part time at a coffee shop while in between jobs.

One Friday afternoon, a strikingly handsome man walked in. He was dressed in a perfect fitting light gray suit and pink shirt. The top three buttons were unbuttoned. His black curly hair was cut short, and his green eyes drew attention to his long eyelashes. Mine wasn't the only head that turned that day.

He walked up to me at the counter and ordered a macchiato. He fiddled and nervously tapped on the counter. As soon as I completed his order, he sat down by the window and stared out at the busy street outside. When I looked up after serving another customer, I noticed he was gone.

For the next month of Fridays, he would return at the same time, always impeccably dressed. The young woman who worked with me on my shift started a friendly competition on who would get to have a conversation with Prince Charming each Friday. As his visits became more regular, he would smile and greet us as he came up to the counter. It was hard not to stare at his remarkable eyes.

One day I asked, "How are you doing today? The usual?" As the coffee shop wasn't busy at the time, I was hoping we could engage in a little conversation.

"Yes, please. And I'm good, thanks. Russell here." He reached out to shake my hand.

Caught off guard by his friendly gesture, I quickly grabbed a towel to wipe my hands and introduced myself. My coworker gave me a jealous frown. I winked back, knowing I had won that round of our competition.

"Do you live in the area, or are you visiting?"

"Business. I come in to town every Friday for a meeting at the county courthouse."

He didn't offer any more conversation, but he kept his

warm smile. Based on his professional dress and courthouse appointments, I assumed he might be an attorney, only to discover much later that my making assumptions only made me the proverbial donkey's ass.

One Friday, Russell came in a bit later than usual. I was just getting off my shift and had changed in to sweatpants for my bike ride back to my apartment. As I was getting ready to leave, my coworker said she had a big order and asked if I would mind taking a sandwich to Russell, who was sitting at his usual table.

"It looks like you're ending your day," Russell said politely as I approached the table.

For a moment I thought he was going to invite me to sit down. My heart was beating rapidly.

"Yep, I have to get home and walk the dog." I thought, *What a stupid response.*

As I turned to walk away, I felt the leg of my sweatpants get caught on something. I pulled my leg away, and Russell jumped.

"Are you OK?" I asked. I didn't know whether to be embarrassed or concerned.

After about ten seconds of uncomfortable silence, he responded, "Uh, hmm, well, your leg got caught on my electronic ankle shackle."

"Ankle shackle?" I tilted my head and added, "I don't understand."

"I'm on electronic monitoring. It's part of my pretrial condition." He paused, trying to avoid making eye contact with me. He added, "I have to report to court every Friday."

"Oh." I didn't know what to say. "I—"

His smile disappeared, and he started tapping his fingers on the table.

"Listen, I'd better go." He quickly grabbed his sandwich and stood up. "I think I've embarrassed both of us."

Before I could say anything, he walked out the door.

I worked at the coffee shop for another month, but Russell never came back. For a long time afterward, the first thing I would do when I met someone was glance at their feet to see if there was anything unusual sticking out from the bottom of their pants.

Sometimes a person can electrify a room by their mere physical presence. Russell gave new meaning to that expression.

"OOPS"—PAULO

Curtis, whom I described earlier as one of my first and most innocent crushes, eventually grew up and got married. My crush ended even though I would always have a warm spot for him. During my last several visits to their farm, his father, Paulo, had taken a liking to me, and I assumed it was largely because of my interest in landscaping and botany. As I observed him, I grew to understand where Curtis had gotten his good looks and personality. Paulo was quintessential Brazilian: dark complexion, short curly black hair, and green eyes. He was very open in his display of physicality, generously offering hugs and holding your arm or shoulder to help punctuate his animated conversation. He had a swagger but never seemed hurried. He appeared to enjoy every moment.

As communication between Curtis and me became

more sporadic, I began to find myself trying to create an excuse to visit again, realizing it was Paulo I was beginning to miss. I felt guilty, thinking that maybe it was inappropriate that I had developed a crush on Curtis's father. After all, it was Curtis whom I'd swooned over privately for years.

My college years passed with little communication with Curtis or Paulo. After graduating, I got a job at a local conservatory for the park district. My boss told me about a seminar at the community college on native Midwest plants, so I decided to sign up. There were more than one hundred attendees, who broke into smaller groups for specialized seminars. I noticed a seminar called Landscaping with Purpose. It sounded interesting, so I signed up and took my seat toward the rear of the small conference room.

I hadn't been in the room more than a couple of minutes when the lecturer entered. It was Paulo!

I shook my head and wiped my eyes. I thought, *Of all the seminars in all the towns of all the world, he walked in to mine.* As I indulged in my brief *Casablanca* moment, I revisited the memories of past visits. I recalled the contrasting images of him, at one moment covered in sweat and dirt while doing his landscaping work, and a few hours later dressed in his chef's apron while slicing vegetables, seasoning a pork roast, and bragging about his Brazilian truffle dessert called *brigadeiro.*

I doubted that Paulo had recognized me sitting in back or noticed my name on the attendee roster. To this day I can't remember a single word of his lecture other than "Welcome to the seminar. My name is Paulo Ribeira."

After class I went to the front, and before I could introduce myself, he rushed toward me, his eyes characteristically squinting from his broad smile. He wrapped his big arms around me.

"It's so good to see you, man. This is such a nice surprise!"

I nervously replied, "Paulo, it's wonderful to see you too. I had no idea you were teaching seminars."

"I only do this a couple of times a year. It gets me off the farm to civilization for a short while."

We laughed.

With little time to chat before his next seminar, he asked, "Say, I'd love you to come back and visit me at the farm. A lot has changed since you were here last. And I'll make you a great meal!" He winked.

Without hesitation, I said, "Yes, I'd love to."

I squeezed the pen I was holding so tight that it left a mark on the palm of my hand. We exchanged phone numbers.

For several weeks Paulo and I exchanged phone calls. The nervousness went away, and I started to feel the same comfort as I had years ago. We'd reminisce and laugh at silly stories such as the time some of Curtis's goats ate the plants meant for one of Paulo's clients. Paulo said Curtis and his wife had opened their new veterinary hospital adjacent to the farm.

Eventually, we settled on a date for me to visit.

A month later, I was exiting the familiar highway off-ramp that still proclaimed No Services This Exit. Entering the long gravel driveway to the farm, I passed Curtis's newly built Ribeira Veterinary Clinic, a pen of goats, and several shiny new landscaping trucks with the Ribeira logo.

My excitement grew as I drove up the driveway. A young golden retriever ran out to greet me. Comet the Lab had passed, and Paulo said he would never be without a dog in the house. I always liked that about him.

As I reached the porch, Paulo walked out the front door wearing his signature smile. He said, "It's great to see you!" He gave me a bear hug.

Again, his intoxicating scent swept over me, a natural mix of sweat and the coconut conditioner in his hair.

I could also tell there was something cooking in the kitchen.

"Something smells great—besides you, Paulo!" I was instantly embarrassed for having said exactly what I was thinking.

"I'm making a special dinner for you, including—"

I interrupted, asking, "Brigadeiro?"

He laughed. "Of course! I want this to be a special visit."

I could barely contain my excitement.

When I walked into the kitchen, Curtis was sitting on a stool by the counter. He jumped up and gave me a hug. "Wow, it's been a long time. How have you been?"

While it was great to see him, I had selfishly hoped to have had 100 percent of Paulo's attention. I replied, "I'm great, Curtis. What a nice surprise to see you! I'm busy working in the city for the park district. And, hey, congratulations on your marriage. And the new clinic looks impressive!"

At that moment, a young woman appeared from another room. I said, "Oh, you must be Curtis's wife. Nice to—"

Curtis interrupted. "Oh no, my wife is at the clinic. This is Angela, my dad's fiancée."

If disappointment could have made a sound that day, then mine would have shattered glass for miles.

*   *   *

Sometimes in the search for romance, you hope for a joyful accident. Although they never seem to happen when you want them to, the universe occasionally finds a way to surprise you.

I confess, I still carry the burden of several secret crushes. But today's Magic 8 Ball says, "outlook not so good."

SWEET ALICE

*A*LICE WAS STARTLED BY A loud clunking sound outside. She looked out the mudroom window and noticed that the shovel she had leaned against the garage had blown over in the wind. She stared at the muddy footprints her boots had left on the sidewalk moments earlier. Stepping back, she saw a reflection in the window. She didn't recognize herself—a gaunt face framed by tangled gray hair with dark rings around her eyes. Her cheeks were scarred from what appeared to be scratch marks. She looked down at the muddy boots she was still wearing. A moment later, she opened the door to the basement stairway.

*   *   *

Just a couple of weeks earlier, Alice Meeks had enjoyed working in her garden. She was the envy of her garden club, and friends often stopped by to admire her flowers and garden art. She had whimsical gnome statues scattered about, a large Zen garden bell, and an antique sundial. When asked what her gardening secret was, she would answer, "It's the gnomes!" They called her Sweet Alice because she would offer visitors coffee and homemade baked goods and she enjoyed showing them around the garden, often giving out cuttings of her favorite plants.

She was an attractive middle-aged widow with an "everyone's grandmother" look, and her kindness and generosity were appreciated by all her fellow club members, with the exception of Trudy Gilson.

Trudy was a bitter widow whose late husband had been convicted of bank fraud. She was the type of person who would lead a protest against anything that was the slightest bit unsavory. She walked with an erect royal posture, her chin raised up as if preparing to summon her subjects. Trudy was insanely jealous of the attention Alice received from the other members. She thought her garden deserved the same attention. She once tried to sabotage one of Alice's flowers in the dahlia competition. She even accused her of bribing judges. Although Alice wasn't the vengeful type, she often wished Trudy would leave the club and go elsewhere. The only time Alice was really hurt was when Trudy made up a story about Alice's deceased husband having an affair with his secretary. For that, Alice never forgave her.

Always on the hunt for unusual things for the garden, Alice frequented garage sales and one day stopped by a house with a For Sale sign in front. It also had a prominent sign in the driveway that read, Urgent Moving Sale. She couldn't resist.

While inspecting the tables, which were covered with typical garage sale items, Alice asked the owner, "What's the urgency about your sale?"

The owner replied, "Well, please don't share this, but I had only been here three months when I seemed to be cursed with bad luck. I love the house, but I've had a string of accidents. I nearly sliced off a finger while working in the garden, and a stone was spit from the lawnmower and hit me in the face." She pointed to the bruise still evident near her eye.

She continued, "And the final straw was a fall down the basement stairs. I decided I'm better off in a condominium."

Alice said, "I'm so sorry. But perhaps you're right. Maintaining a house and yard can be a lot of work."

As Alice continued to inspect the sale items, she noticed what appeared to be a small mud-covered statue lying on its side by the trash can. It was so dirty that she wasn't able to immediately identify what it was. As she wiped away some of the dirt, she discovered it was a gnome of some sort.

"Is this for sale?" Alice asked, pointing to the statue.

The owner replied, "Ugh, you mean that ugly thing? Please take it! I've been meaning to get rid of it since I first found it. I always felt its eyes were following me. I dug it up when planting my geraniums. That's when I nearly chopped off my finger."

As the woman turned around, she bumped one of the tables and a vase fell off and landed on her foot. "Ouch!" she yelled. "See what I mean?"

Alice left thinking the poor woman was probably just clumsy. She was delighted with her garage sale discovery and was eager to add it to her family of gnomes.

When she got home, she carefully scraped off the dirt and gave it a good rinsing. What she uncovered surprised her. It was indeed a gnome of some type, but not the friendly, cuddly, bearded sort most commonly seen in gardens like her own. This one was squat with a flat head. Instead of the usual tall pointed hat, it wore a large leaf on its head. Its large, irregularly shaped ears did nothing to distract from the somber face, which included squinting eyes and a frown that was a bit chilling if stared at for too long. Nevertheless, Alice thought it unusual and put it on the top shelf of her garden bench next to one of her other, more congenial-looking gnomes.

It was only a few days later when Alice started having minor accidents that were atypical for someone so experienced in the garden. She cut her finger and even tripped over a flowerpot that somehow had fallen off its stand. At night, she started having nightmares. She would wake up with unexplained scratches on her arms, and then later on her face. One night during a nightmare, she stabbed herself with a pen that was on her nightstand. The lack of sleep and the stress took its toll. She wasn't eating well, and her mental state began to deteriorate. She withdrew from her friends and stopped attending garden club meetings. She ignored the repeated attempts by her friends to contact her.

One evening after a heavy storm, Alice walked outside to check on her garden. She had grown weak and disoriented. She noticed one of her favorite gnomes had fallen off the bench and shattered. Thinking she heard a voice, she turned around and looked at the gnomes lined up on the garden bench.

"Stop staring at me!" she yelled at the somber-looking garage sale gnome. Thinking that it was responsible for pushing the other gnome off the bench, she became enraged.

She quickly got a shovel, grabbed the offensive gnome, and buried it.

She returned to the mudroom, wet and dazed, and was about to take off her muddy boots. A moment later, she opened the door to the basement stairway. After just one step, she tumbled down the stairs to the cement floor of the landing. She was not as fortunate as the woman at the garage sale who had sold her the gnome.

Alice was discovered days later after the mailman reported a pile of unopened mail. Her funeral was attended by many of her admirers. Trudy did not attend.

In her will, Alice donated her house to the town with the stipulation it would be razed and replaced by a children's park.

A month later, the garden club built a small memorial garden in front of the town library as a tribute to Alice. They called it the "Sweet Alice Garden." The club members held a short memorial service when it opened. Again, Trudy did not attend. Instead, while everyone was distracted, she snuck off to Alice's property.

Aware of the request in Alice's will, Trudy wanted to salvage whatever she could from Alice's once thriving garden. When she arrived, she discovered that the bulldozers had already destroyed most everything. Desperate to have a piece of Alice's legacy for herself, she combed through mounds of dirt and noticed a small stone statue covered in mud. Without stopping to inspect her discovery, she grabbed the muddy statue, wrapped it in newspaper, and rushed back home.

Karma couldn't have chosen a better souvenir for Trudy to abscond with. While her demise came quickly, the legacy of that gnome persevered long after Trudy's fatal fall from her second-floor balcony. Over the years, the gnome would "accidentally" find its way in to other gardens. An unexplained increase in fatal falls haunted the town.

A decade passed. One of the newer members of the garden club had heard all the praise about the legendary Alice—her awards, her beautiful garden, and the collection of gnomes and garden art. One day while at a swap meet, she found an old gnome and thought it was as unique as was Alice in her gardening talent. She had no room for it in her townhouse but thought that adding the gnome to the Sweet Alice Garden by the library would be a fitting way to honor the late gardener.

For months afterward, paramedics routinely were called to the library as a result of people falling down the front steps.

The cause of a fire that consumed the library later that year was never determined.

WAUKENA FALLS

AUKENA FALLS WAS A TINY town, barely a rest stop on a highway leading to the northern woods of Wisconsin. With a population straining to reach twelve hundred, it wasn't known for much other than having the distinction of being located at 45 degrees latitude, or halfway between the equator and the North Pole. The cement-styled tree stump monument in the town square proudly celebrated this geographic feature with a commemorative plaque. But amid the pastoral landscape of dairy land was concealed a little-known story more sinister than Waukena's harmless geography lesson.

It was 1955 and Trevor Morgan, a feature writer for the *County Register*, the county's largest newspaper, had come across an old newspaper clipping while researching another story. The clipping made mention of a tragic fire and murder in nearby Waukena Falls almost thirty years ago. Always looking for a new story, Trevor was determined to dig a little deeper.

Not easily intimidated, Trevor pressed a number of the

town's residents to see if they knew of anything odd that had happened in Waukena Falls decades ago. No one expressed any knowledge of such a crime or at least didn't want to admit they knew anything. Their reluctance served only to add to Trevor's motivation to learn more.

One day while unsuccessfully canvassing some of the town's residents, Trevor came across an old man sitting in front of the tavern. Seeing that the man was struggling to light his pipe, Trevor offered him his lighter. After chatting a bit, Trevor discovered that the old man knew something about an event that seemed similar to what was described in the old newspaper clipping.

The scruffy bearded man spoke in short sentences but seemed pleased that someone had taken some interest in him. He introduced himself as Mack. After offering him lunch and a beer, Trevor sat and listened patiently, grateful that Mack spoke slowly but in amazing detail. After several hours and as many beers, Trevor was intrigued. After going back to his office and compiling his notes, he wondered if he had stumbled upon a big secret of Waukena Falls.

According to Mack, it was the 1920s and logging was at its peak. Waukena Falls was a bustling little town, home to loggers and the nearest source of supplies for the many small farmers who populated the area. Among the dry goods store and the mandatory barbershop, saloon, and hotel, there had been an unusual business at the end of Main Street. Mack said the store sold lightning rods. While many residents of Waukena Falls had no idea what this new contraption was, some of the local farmers with large barns had heard about lightning rods and were interested in learning more.

The proprietor of the store was not a local. Mr. Winslow,

a sophisticated young man from Milwaukee, arrived in Waukena Falls quite by accident. He had answered an ad requesting information about lightning rods for use on the local barns and farmhouses. Lightning rods provided a practical solution by deflecting dangerous lightning strikes from property, as well as being an attractive addition to any building. The plain six-foot copper rods were each mounted on a short metal tripod on the roof and grounded with a thick copper cable running down the side of the building to the ground. The thick copper cable did the heavy lifting of deflecting a hot bolt of lightning from the structure to the ground. Many rods were adorned with glass balls of many shapes and colors, as well as with fancy weathervane arrows. Trevor later discovered that lightning rods and their adornments had become quite collectible by antique dealers.

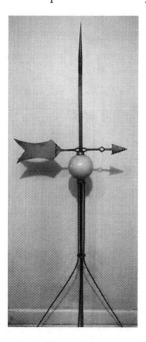

After arriving in Waukena Falls, Winslow found interest great enough that he decided to open a permanent shop where he could display and sell the rods. He moved his son and daughter from the city to join him, much against their wishes.

Mack said that Winslow made lots of money the first several years, until something tragic happened. One afternoon, a fierce line of thunderstorms raced through northern Wisconsin. Weather records documented the storm as an intense episode of incredible lightning, wind, and rain. At the time, the lightning rods Winslow had sold numbered in the dozens. After the storms passed, word spread of numerous house and barn fires at the site of many of his lightning rod installations. His clientele quickly turned on him and blamed him for the extensive loss of property. It turned out that Winslow, a bit of a hustler, never provided the necessary copper cables to his unknowing clients, leaving the installed lightning rods as nothing more than useless ornaments. At this point Trevor was amazed at Mack's detailed recollections. He wondered if he was just being told a tale for attention.

Mack continued. He explained that justice back then was local and served by vigilantes rather than a courtroom. A group of angry townspeople dragged Winslow from his store, and one irate farmer took one of the lightning rods from the store and drove it through Winslow's chest. His store was burned to the ground, and all the lightning rod paraphernalia was buried in an unmarked grave with Winslow's body. It was August 1928. His children were never seen again and supposedly fled town to head back to the city.

It was at this point in his interview that Mack paused and shook his head. Trevor asked what was wrong, but Mack slowly sipped his beer and looked out the tavern window. Trevor suspected there was more to the story. Mack's sudden hesitancy only increased Trevor's journalistic curiosity. He knew with persistence that the truth would eventually come to light.

Even though Trevor found it difficult to corroborate Mack's story, he figured it would at least be an entertaining feature for the paper.

Eager to meet a publication deadline, Trevor took only one evening to write his feature article. However, because of other events that week, including a large forest fire and the birth of quadruplets, his story got buried and was never published until he returned to continue his investigation five years later.

It was 1960. Ethan was a fifteen-year-old nerdy schoolboy who was ridiculed by other kids for his thick-lensed glasses, his lack of interest in sports, and his obsession with reading. He didn't particularly excel in schoolwork except for his love of science. He lived alone with his widowed mother, Francis, whom many townspeople believed was mad and obsessed with demonic spirits.

Ethan did his best to ignore the crazy rantings of his mother and buried himself in his books as an escape. He often went down to their cellar for privacy and quiet. One afternoon, he looked up in the rafters and saw a large pole protruding from some loose boards. The pole looked unusual in that it was pointed on one end and its copper finish had oxidized to a dull green. He stood on his chair and started to pull. The pole was six feet long. He looked among the boards and saw what appeared to be a tripod of iron legs, which he pulled down as well. After one more look up in the rafters, he saw a large box and managed to gently lower it to the floor. He laid all his recent discoveries on the floor and started to assemble what was indeed an old lightning rod. Once the rod was upright in the stand, he added the red glass ball and directional arrow. He wasn't sure at first what it was, but then he recalled in one of his science books having seen a drawing of a lightning deflector that had a similar design.

Ethan noticed that an old fragment of newsprint had fallen out of the box. He picked it up and read the yellowed and barely legible paper. It was an obituary, but he could only make out part of it:

> Au – – – st 14, 192 –, decea – sed
> H– – – – M– – – – – –, a.k.a Mr. Jim
> Wins – ow
> Surviv – – by his – – – – – – – – – – –
> Fran – is and son Mack – – zie

A few days later, Ethan's mother's mood turned violent when she discovered that he had found the lightning rod and assembled it on the roof of the shed in back of the house. When he asked her about the obituary, she went into a rage and chased him throughout the house, threatening to beat him. As they neared the stairway to the basement, they struggled. She tumbled down the stairs and hit her head on the cement floor of the landing. Ethan didn't call the police, fearing they would think he purposely killed his mother. He buried her body in the backyard.

It was several months later, and Ethan had just gone to bed. He heard distant rumbles of thunder. The storm intensified quickly, and within minutes the lightning flashed almost continuously. Suddenly, there was one loud crack and a bright flash, followed by a huge explosion that blew out some of the windows. He was thrown to his feet and temporarily knocked out. When he woke up, he heard people yelling outside his house. He cautiously opened the back door and saw a group of people standing around a crater about eight feet across and several feet deep. He walked to the edge and peered down into the hole. While the debris in the hole wasn't easily recognizable by the other observers, Ethan knew exactly what it was. The bent, charred rods of copper and the broken glass of several colors were parts to lightning rods. Lightning had hit the shed where he had mounted his lightning rod and ignited a nearby propane tank, which exploded.

One of the onlookers climbed in to the hole and pushed aside several copper rods and pieces of broken glass. After a few moments he yelled, "Oh, good God! There are human bones in here."

After forensics inspected the remains and some clothing, it was determined they belonged to one Jim Winslow, the owner of the lightning rod business, and his daughter Francis, Ethan's mother.

A week later, Ethan walked into the county sheriff's office and confessed, telling the story of the struggle he had had with his mother. He shared the partial obituary, and authorities confirmed that Mack was Jim Winslow's son and Francis's brother.

At the start of Ethan's trial, prosecutors withdrew the

most serious charges and reduced them to one: involuntary manslaughter. Ethan was eventually released on probation. As a witness, Mack revealed that Francis had betrayed their father when the angry mob descended on his lightning rod shop thirty years ago. Out of spite for having forced her to move to Waukena Falls, she told the angry mob that her father purposely had neglected to tell them about the copper cable required to make the lightning rods functional. In their anger, they killed Jim Winslow. Francis later started to lose her mind over her guilt.

Mack explained he had used the insurance money from the lightning rod store to build a small house for his sister on the site of the destroyed shop. Francis married, but shortly after Ethan was born her husband left, complaining that Francis's mind wasn't right. Mack was later ostracized by the townspeople. He began to drink heavily and lived his life in seclusion above the tavern.

Trevor Morgan was now senior editor of the *County Register*. He wanted to interview Mack again, but the old man had passed away suddenly after the trial. Before publishing his story, Trevor decided to go back to the boardinghouse above the tavern where Mack lived to see if he could find anything revealing. The police had already inspected it, but Trevor wanted one last look.

The apartment was sparse, just a single bed, a small desk, and a chair. Trevor opened the desk drawer. It was empty. When he pushed the drawer back, it wouldn't shut. He took the drawer out and inspected it. On the bottom was a small aged piece of newsprint. It was the full copy of the obituary that Ethan had found in his basement. It read:

August 14, 1928, deceased
Henry Morgan, a.k.a Mr. Jim Winslow
Survived by his daughter Francis and son
Mackenzie

Trevor sat on the bare mattress in Mack's room in deep thought. He hadn't recalled anyone within miles who shared his last name, Morgan. He wondered if by some slim chance he was related to Henry Morgan. Trevor had grown up in a foster home and was told his mother died when he was a baby and his father wasn't able to care for him.

Trevor was under pressure to publish the story, but privately he pursued an investigation into his own childhood and a search for his father. He investigated for years without learning any more about his possible relationship to Henry Morgan or of his father's true identity. Unfortunately, DNA testing wasn't yet available, and Trevor died without ever knowing who his father really was.

Years later, a young journalist from Milwaukee read Trevor's article while doing his own research on cold cases in Wisconsin. He was intrigued by Trevor's search for his real father. With DNA testing finally available, he was able to get the court to exhume the remains of Henry Morgan, Mack, Francis, and Trevor. After comparing their DNA, it was determined that Trevor was Mack's son. The young journalist published an updated version of Trevor's original story.

As news of the story spread, a renewed energy returned to the streets of Waukena Falls. Tourists went out of their way to see the new lightning rod museum. An especially popular spot for photos was a new memorial across the street from the old tree stump monument. It was a plain concrete pedestal with a plaque that read, "Dedicated to all the farmers of Waukena Falls."

Mounted on top of the pedestal was a six-foot copper—well, you know.

IF

MANY PEOPLE ARE PERFECTLY HAPPY with the life choices they've made. Others wonder what their lives would have been like if only they had made different decisions. Clay was a member of the What-If Club.

Since retirement, Clay had had time to reflect. He had what most would have considered an accomplished and successful career. He rose to senior management in a major company, lived and worked overseas, and even wrote a cookbook based on recipes he had collected while living in Central America. While he was generally satisfied, he often felt he had lived someone else's life instead of pursuing his own. He wondered what his life would have been like if he had chosen a different path. What if the universe had chosen one coincidence over another?

In fourth grade, when his class was asked what they wanted to be when they grew up, most of the young boys responded with the expected answers of fireman, doctor, or airplane pilot. Clay claimed he wished to pursue the auspicious career of motel owner.

When he was in college, he still had little idea of what he wanted to do. He envied those classmates who knew exactly which careers they wanted to pursue. Although he liked plants and horticulture, he defaulted to a major in history.

After graduation, Clay remained rudderless. While he was at a family reunion, an uncle happened to mention an open position at his bank. Coincidence won out.

What happened to Clay happens to many people. He let chance guide his future.

Lewis Carroll wrote, "If you don't know where you're going, then any road will take you there." Such was Clay's life journey.

One night Clay was awakened by a familiar voice. His room was dark except for the light from his clock radio. As soon as he recognized the figure in the shadows, he sat up in bed and yelled, "Oh my God, what happened? Did I die?"

"Calm down, Clay," the comforting voice said. "It's me. ... I mean, it's you—Young Clay of fifty-one years ago."

Clay chanted to himself, "Wake up, Clay. Wake up. This must be a dream."

Young Clay responded, "Yes, this is a dream. But don't worry. I'm here for a purpose. I'm to tell you that we have had a good life and we should be grateful for that."

"Hold on a minute, young me. Are you a ghost of Christmas past or something?" Clay was still dazed and trying to get used to "we."

Young Clay laughed. "Oh no, not a ghost. Probably more like a genie with some special powers. I'm part of your conscience, trying to clear up some anxieties about whether we really lived the life we wanted."

"Hmm, that's a relief," Clay answered sarcastically. He added, "And can we stop with the 'we' business? It's sort of freaking me out."

Young Clay continued, "OK then, what if *I* had made different choices when presented with various opportunities in those early days? I had an interest in plants, botany, and working outdoors in nature. But something kept me from pursuing any of those interests."

Clay responded, "Well, it's too late to change anything now."

"Of course. And this visit isn't to figure out why I made various decisions but rather to give you some peace of mind by looking back and answering some of your doubts about the turns your—our—life has taken." Young Clay tried to reassure his older self that he wasn't there to judge him for past decisions.

"OK, I guess I have no choice. And I do admit I've had time now in retirement to look back at my life, and I have asked myself those very questions." Clay's nerves still hadn't settled, but he knew he couldn't wake up until the dream was over.

Young Clay began, "Kierkegaard, whom *I* studied in college philosophy class, said, 'Life can only be understood backward, but it must be lived forward.'" He explained, "I'm going to take you backward and look at some of the regrets you have about the choices I made when I was young. I know you look back and think that because of these choices, you denied yourself the life you really wanted. I'm going to show you that perhaps you have lived the life that was meant for you and that there is still time to achieve some of your other youthful dreams."

He sat down on the dresser across the bed from where Clay was still lying and continued, saying, "I'm going to summon some of that special power I have and take you on several short journeys." He chuckled and added, "You know, one always has special powers in dreams."

Despite what felt like an out-of-body experience, Clay's curiosity overcame his nerves about talking with himself. He listened carefully as Young Clay did a fast rewind through the first what-if scenario.

Young Clay snapped his fingers, and all of a sudden Clay felt that he was inside a snow globe. The walls of his bedroom disappeared, and a fog surrounded him. Young Clay sat next to him on the bed.

"OK, let's begin and return to college. In this scenario, what if I, Young Clay, had majored in botany instead of history? After graduation, I joined the Peace Corps and helped farmers develop sustainable crops in equatorial Africa. Of course, unpleasant things could have happened, such as catching malaria, but I'm not going to focus on the bad stuff."

While Young Clay was describing the scenario, foggy images of him working in a field in Africa appeared across the room.

Young Clay continued, "Upon my return, I got a master's and then a PhD in horticulture and taught at a major university until retirement."

Clay was looking a little puzzled throughout the quick trip back in time, unsure how he should react.

Young Clay said, "Let's move on to another scenario.

Let's say I actually realized my fourth grade dream of being a motel owner. Well, sort of. I raised the bar by actually opening my own bed-and-breakfast. I found the work of hospitality rewarding and fun. I eventually married a partner who shared the same joy of running an inn. I was able to incorporate my love of gardening by creating adjoining gardens that eventually became attractions in their own right."

Clay watched another faint image of him welcoming guests at an inn. He interrupted, "But how do you know all of this?"

Young Clay smiled. "Don't question my superpowers. And give me a break, it's a dream!" He continued. "Because of my love of plants and the outdoors, in this next career scenario I joined the National Forest Service right after college. It wasn't exactly a parent-pleasing career choice, but I was excited about the adventure and work outdoors. My first assignment was in Death Valley National Park, a universally dreaded assignment designed to cull the weaker rookies. I endured and graduated to friendlier climes such as Yellowstone, Zion, and ultimately Olympic National Park in Washington as senior park ranger. My adventures were many, and I became part of a close-knit community of rangers and firefighters. The one thing missing was a secure family life. I was in a relationship for only a short time. The moving and remote locations required a partner who shared the same adventurous spirit. I was left with a secure but often lonely retirement."

Clay sat up in the bed and was so completely drawn in that he momentarily forgot he was listening to his younger self. He could almost smell the pine forests of Washington that appeared across the room.

Young Clay continued his lesson. "The final scenario is a tough one. I enlisted in the navy after graduation. I had a lower draft lottery number and figured I would be drafted anyway. It was near the end of the Vietnam War, and I was assigned a ship that was sent to patrol the Mekong River. I completed my tour, but some of the horrors and injustices I saw left me scarred and disenchanted with government and politics. I struggled with mediocre and unfulfilling jobs for a couple of years after being discharged. It took the strong support of family and friends to direct me to a career in counseling. I eventually got a master's degree in social work and worked the remainder of my career within the veterans' hospital system. I was rewarded by the support I was able to provide other veterans, and that work also helped me to deal with the effects of my own wartime experiences, some of which haunt me to this day."

Clay was totally silent. He found the images of him counseling broken soldiers in the veterans' hospital to be upsetting.

Young Clay stood up and walked toward the door. "I just gave you four examples, but there are an infinite number of scenarios that could have played out with just small changes to a decision to do something different or not to do something. Socrates said, 'A life not examined is not a life worth living.' In other words, it's normal to reflect on your life, taking credit for the wins and excusing yourself for the shortcomings."

Clay interrupted, "That's sometimes easier—"

Young Clay interrupted, saying, "You know, time can

be slippery thing—sometimes deceitful and cruel, and other times forgiving and reaffirming. One thing is for sure: it's often gone before we can embrace it. In the end, some of those decisions that happened by accident carry with them some of the best memories. Don't look back and wish you could live the cycle again as someone different. Be happy you survived the journey for this long."

Young Clay got up and started to walk away.

Clay said, "But wait—"

Young Clay didn't let him finish. As his image started to fade, he said, "Celebrate it. And keep living. We did good!" The fog in Clay's bedroom cleared. The dream ended, and Clay lay sound asleep.

He got up early the next morning, drowsy and disoriented. He tried to remember details of the unusual dream, but they quickly faded as he started to wake up. He felt different though, as if a burden had been removed. He sipped his morning coffee and noticed a community college catalog was on the kitchen counter. He didn't remember its being there before. It was opened to a page of course listings.

He looked closely. The Botany 100 course was circled in red ink. Next to the course description was a handwritten note: "We did good!"

PINE STREET

"Hey, Munch, we have a 415 at 201 Pine Street," the dispatcher at the Twin Oaks police station instructed soon-to-be-retired Detective Harvey Mumford, asking him to check out a possible disturbance. Harvey's nickname had been Munch ever since officer training camp. It was short for munchkin because he was short and had an odd, squeaky voice. It was his last duty night before retirement, and he was on call. Since it was his final night, dispatch and his squad wanted to play a joke on him, so they sent him out on a fake call.

At one point in his career, Harvey was an honored officer with a record of solved crimes that the younger detectives envied. But his captain noticed a steady decline in Harvey's mental state, and for that reason the detective hadn't been sent out on a call in several months. Harvey had become what they called a "house mouse," used to refer to an officer who didn't go out on patrol or cover crime scenes.

Harvey always had been somewhat of a recluse—widowed when he was young and never having remarried.

He rarely attended precinct social events. Recently he had become more withdrawn at work, and at times he seemed indifferent to his surroundings—not a particularly good trait for a detective. He grew to love his science fiction books more than his detective work and often argued with fellow officers about time travel and reincarnation.

He had once remarked to a former partner, "I feel like I'm living in an era that doesn't exist—either the past or the future, but not the present."

Concerned, the captain eventually brought up the suggestion of retirement. Harvey had earned full retirement benefits, and he agreed it was time.

Harvey drove a squad car down to 201 Pine Street as directed by dispatch. It was a coffee shop, and the lights were on. The front door had a Closed sign in the window, but he noticed the door was ajar. He entered, his hand on his weapon.

"Hello. Twin Oaks police. Anyone here?"

There was no answer. He searched the cafe and found no evidence of anyone there.

When he went behind the counter, he noticed an ID on the floor. It was the driver's license of Gladys Emerson. He put the license in a baggie for evidence and called it in as a 211, a possible robbery. Dispatch called him back and told him it was a joke for his last night and that he should come back to the station.

Harvey was puzzled. *They'd go through this much trouble for a joke?*

He returned to the station, where dispatch and his squad mates broke in to laughter and brought out a cake with candles iced with "Happy Retirement, Munch." They also gave him a plaque thanking him for his service.

Harvey, unamused and not particularly grateful for the cake, insisted that something strange must have occurred at the coffee shop on Pine Street. He handed the captain the driver's license he had found.

The captain told Harvey, "OK, Munch, you got even with us. Now, let's eat cake and you can relax on your last shift."

Harvey insisted, "No, Captain. I'm not kidding."

Everyone laughed. "Munch, let it go, ole man. You got us back good. You know there's no coffee shop there. It's just an empty lot," one officer yelled.

But Harvey insisted.

Officer Emery was one of Harvey's few friends on the force. His shift was ending. He said, "Hey, Munch, I promise to drive by Pine Street on my way home and check it out."

Meanwhile, one of the other detectives tried to find information about Gladys Emerson. He couldn't find anything more about her other than the address on the driver's license.

The captain added, "One of you guys drive by Emerson's address tomorrow and return her license, OK?" He paused. "And ask her if she remembers where she lost it."

Harvey was frustrated with all the jokes. He turned his badge in and said his goodbyes.

The next day at the precinct, there was concern that Officer Emery hadn't reported in for his shift. They called his wife, who said he never came home that night. She had assumed he had to work a double shift.

That same day, one of the officers drove to Gladys

Emerson's address. He knocked on the door of her apartment. The door was ajar.

"Hello, Ms. Emerson? Twin Oaks police."

After no response, the officer entered the apartment. It was completely empty—no furniture, nothing on the walls. The kitchen was empty—no sign of life.

As he was ready to leave, he noticed a piece of paper on the kitchen counter. It was a receipt from the Pine Street Coffee House, 201 Pine Street.

Confused, he rushed out of the apartment and headed back to the precinct.

Later that same day the captain drove to Harvey's house to deliver the service plaque that he had forgotten at the precinct the night before. Knocking on the door, which he noticed was ajar, he walked in yelling, "Harvey, it's Captain—" Before he could finish, he stopped, stunned at what he saw. The house was completely empty. No sign of Harvey, only a receipt on the kitchen counter from the Pine Street Coffee House, 201 Pine Street.

None of the mysteries were ever solved: the phantom coffee house, or the missing Officer Emery, Gladys, or Harvey.

From that day forward, not a single officer from the precinct would drive by that corner on Pine Street.

A month later a new detective was hired to replace Harvey and was assigned his old desk. The captain came by to welcome him to the precinct.

"Mm," the captain said. "That coffee smells so good. Where did you get it from?"

As the young detective held up the coffee cup the Captain backed away suddenly as if he had seen a ghost. The name printed on the cup was Pine Street Coffee House.

AUTHOR'S NOTE

Back in the day my mother would tell me, "You can go outside and do whatever you want. Just be home by dark." That childhood freedom, seemingly in short supply these days, taught me and many of my peers about independence and self-confidence.

Those qualities led me to experience countless adventures and relationships, and joys and sorrows, all of which informed these stories.

All of us live our own "short stories," revealing our truth through some combination of fact and fantasy. As I sit in my local coffee house writing this afterword, I wonder about the short stories being "written" by all the people around me enjoying their lattes. But it's getting late, and Gladys Emerson just offered me a ride. I want to be home before dark.

Printed in the United States
by Baker & Taylor Publisher Services